SOMEONE TO WATCH OVER YOU

T0384470

KUMI KIMURA is a Japanese writer. She won the Literary World Newcomer Award for her debut novel, and has subsequently been shortlisted twice for the Akutagawa Prize and won the Bunkamura Deux Magots Literary Prize. *Someone to Watch Over You* is her first work to be translated into English.

YUKI TEJIMA is a translator from Los Angeles who is currently based in Tokyo. Her translations include *Lost Souls Meet Under a Full Moon* and *How to Hold Someone in Your Heart* by Mizuki Tsujimura, *Then Why'd You Ask Me To Come?* by Risa Wataya, and *Totto-chan, the Little Girl at the Window: The Sequel* by Tetsuko Kuroyanagi.

SOMEONE TO WATCH OVER YOU

KUMI KIMURA

Translated from the Japanese by

YUKI TEJIMA

Pushkin Press
Somerset House, Strand
London WC2R 1LA

Someone to Watch Over You was first published as *Anata ni anzen
na hito* by KAWADE SHOBO SHINSHA Ltd. in Tokyo, 2021

First published by Pushkin Press in 2025

Series Editors: David Karashima and Michael Emmerich
Translation Editor: Elmer Luke

Pushkin Press would like to thank the Yanai Initiative for Globalizing
Japanese Humanities at UCLA and Waseda University for its support.

◼︎ YANAI INITIATIVE

ISBN 13: 978-1-80533-005-9

Designed and typeset by Tetragon, London
Printed and bound in the United Kingdom by Clays Ltd, Elcograf S.p.A.

EU RP (for authorities only): eucomply OÜ, Pärnu mnt. 139b-14, 11317,
Tallinn, Estonia, hello@eucompliancepartner.com, +33757690241

Pushkin Press is committed to a sustainable future for our
business, our readers and our planet. This book is made from
paper from forests that support responsible forestry.

MIX
Paper | Supporting
responsible forestry
FSC® C018072

www.pushkinpress.com

1 3 5 7 9 8 6 4 2

SOMEONE TO WATCH OVER YOU

On a cold April afternoon, Tae, who was still in her pajamas, with a padded *hanten* over her shoulders, had just finished her lunch when the doorbell rang.

"Hello, um, I'm here to check your bathtub," said a squeaky voice over the intercom.

She looked at her calendar. "Isn't the appointment for tomorrow?" she asked.

"No, you're down for today. I'm booked tomorrow and for the next few days."

She rushed to her front door, grabbing the paper bag that had been sitting unopened next to a vase of flowers on the shoe cabinet. "Just a moment," she called through the door before hurrying upstairs to her room, where she put on a pair of corduroys, a tattered turtleneck, and a sweater, then affixed her cloth face mask.

Going back downstairs, she looked into the bathroom to be sure all was spick-and-span. Like the rest of the house, it was perfect—what with her using only a broom, duster, and rags once her vacuum cleaner broke at the start of the year. After seeing the endless footage of mud- and kelp-drenched television sets everywhere following the tsunami, she'd sworn off any new electronics.

"I'm sorry to keep you waiting," she said as she opened the front door. "Thank you for coming." The handyman was a head taller than her and looked a dozen years younger than her forty-six years. He was wearing eyeglasses and a gray mask wrapped around his jaw.

"It's this way," Tae said, as the man stepped into the brown slippers he had brought with him and followed her into the house. "The problem started last week. The water won't drain when I go to empty the tub." She led him to the wet room—which had a bathtub and washing area next to it—where a faint light floated in through the small, frosted window.

Tae had lived in this house only since the last year. She had moved back to town after nine exhausting years in Tokyo, when her mother was hospitalized for malignant lymphoma. Her mother didn't make it through the summer, and in the fall her father died of a heart attack. So the house was now hers. Each day, she painstakingly removed every last stray hair from the bathroom drains with duct tape. Once in a while she'd notice an unpleasant sewage odor, but she ignored it. She tried not to think about the darkness on the other side.

She wanted to tell the man that the clog wasn't her fault, but she also didn't need to make excuses to someone she would never see again.

"I'll get started then," the man said, dashing back to his car and returning with some equipment, including a plunger and a bucket.

"Thank you," Tae mumbled and went to her room, where she opened the paper bag that she had left untouched for two weeks. It was from the man from Tokyo.

The gift box inside was covered in a sheet of *noshi*, with calligraphy that read:

Best wishes, H. Honma

Tae peeled off the *noshi* and yellow-green wrapping to find a rectangular black tin container with a lightning pattern. She opened the lid and lifted off first the layer of bubble wrap, then the sheet of tissue paper, to find an assortment of individual packets of senbei. Some rice crackers were wrapped in nori, and others were speckled with black sesame or sugar crystals. In each packet was a tiny envelope of silica gel.

Curious about the handyman's progress with the drain, Tae held her breath and tiptoed halfway down the stairs. She listened to the sludge of tangled hair and grime from the bodies of her family members through the years being pumped out of the drain and extracted with a pop, like a hit off a bat.

The man occasionally let out a whistle—*hoo, hoo, hoooo*—to the rhythm of marching army boots. Tae could feel his disdain, could hear him thinking: "This woman is so lazy. Living alone, unable to keep things clean. *Especially* these easily overlooked spots." She went back to her room.

She was staring at the senbei on her desk when a triumphant voice called out, "Think I'm done here!" sending a jolt up her spine. She plodded down the stairs and peered into the wet room. The man's gray mask was now black with sweat. He nodded at her, turned on the shower and pointed the nozzle toward the drain.

Wordlessly, the two watched as the stream of water landed on the pale blue tiles before being swallowed into the deep black hole of the drain. Over the sound of the shower, which was like rain at the start of a storm, Tae could hear their breathing overlap. Suddenly self-conscious, she started to perspire, though she'd barely moved a muscle.

Tae paid the handyman his due in an envelope, and, as he was tucking it into his pocket, she handed him the bag. "This is a gift I received," she said. "Will you take it?"

"Are you sure?" he replied, as he pulled the tin of senbei out. Setting the empty bag down, he pried open the lid of the tin, then pulled off the bubble wrap and tissue, and proceeded to plunk himself down on the front door mat. Tae instinctively stepped backward toward the living room as he tore open a packet, pulled out a palm-sized nori-wrapped senbei, yanked his mask down to his chin, and took a big bite. The cracker had gotten a little stale, from the sound of it, but he chomped through it anyway, crumbs spilling from his half-parted lips.

A low moan not unlike a wild animal's escaped from him, and Tae stared. Feeling her eyes on him, the man turned, bent over, then suddenly started coughing. And then choking. The senbei had gotten caught in his throat. "Water, water," he managed to whisper.

Tae rushed into the kitchen and quickly filled a glass from the tap. Placing it next to the hunched man who was now heaving, she inched back across the hallway to resume her position by the living room.

"Thank you," the man wheezed, and gulped down the water. She got him another glass. When he finished it and seemed to be all right, he stood up and bowed. "I'm sorry, I'm very sorry, I do apologize," he said over and over. "I haven't had anything to eat... for three days. I should have been... more careful... with the senbei. I'll buy some food on the way home."

"Yes, please do," Tae murmured, her back glued to the living room door.

The man bowed again, the tin in his hands. Then, squinting at Tae, he said, "I'm guessing you saw my postcard, and that's why you called me... but why? Isn't there someone closer to you?"

"Uh, yes, I don't... I didn't think about it."

"Well, I thank you. Oh, but since I'm here... I heard about the guy from Tokyo... the old guy who died mysteriously the other day... at the dry cleaner's just down the hill from here. Please be careful." Bowing deeply, he turned and left.

Moments later, Tae heard the roar of his engine grow distant.

Tae in fact *had* been thinking about that old guy from Tokyo.

Precisely a week earlier, at around noon, when the chilly weather had returned and she couldn't get out of bed, she heard a piercing siren slice through the air and come to a stop near the dry cleaner's. She had a bad feeling. Keeping her storm shutters closed and the lights turned off, she'd remained in her room for the rest of the afternoon.

She could hear someone going up and down the creaky steel staircase of the dry cleaner's building until sundown, though maybe she imagined that.

Tae had not left her house in a few days, having enough food and necessities at home. She finally stepped out yesterday afternoon and walked by Blue Sky Dry Cleaning, where she saw the same tired bench that had always sat in front of the store. There were no KEEP OUT signs, nor was anything roped off, but she noted that the mail slot on the upstairs apartment door was sealed with blue tape, the same as it had been before Honma moved in. In the short time he lived there, Tae had never seen him come or go; she wouldn't have recognized him if she passed him on the street. Since she never left her house at night, she didn't know if his lights were ever on.

The old guy who died mysteriously.

Tae switched on the TV and watched two afternoon talk shows she had no interest in, then rose to her feet. She opened all the windows and sprayed disinfectant in the spaces the handyman had occupied, wiping down the doorknobs. By the time she finished her laundry, the sun was starting to set.

She had a small serving of rice left in the freezer, so she decided that dinner would be *ochazuke* with *umeboshi*, along with a dish of steamed carrots, daikon, and taro, which she dipped in miso she had made herself. As she slurped on her *ochazuke*, it occurred to her that a soupy dish like this might have been easier to swallow and digest for someone who hadn't eaten in three days. All she could think about at the time, of course, was getting him out of the door as quickly as possible.

*

Shinobu had learned about the Blue Sky Dry Cleaning incident the night before on an anonymous online forum where prefecture residents posted gossip. He noticed that the dry cleaner's in question—the address was there for all to see—was near the house he was scheduled to visit the following day. When he got there, the clogged drain he'd been called to fix didn't require much maintenance. He took his time, knowing he had no reason to hurry.

The woman who'd thrust the gift of senbei on him—the tin had the label of a shop in Ginza—was wearing a plum-blossom-patterned cloth mask that looked hand-sewn. She had thick glasses and the pale skin of someone who hadn't seen the sun in months, reminding him of a paperclay doll.

HIDEKI HONMA OF SETAGAYA WARD, AGE 69

The man was rumored to have died by hanging himself, or maybe it was carbon monoxide, or could it have been slit wrists in the bathtub? He was derided by everybody for having moved here in the first place. He shared a name with Shinobu's former boss at the cleaning company where he used to work. They were about the same age, though the boss was from Adachi Ward in Tokyo.

A former pharmacist. Unmarried, no immediate family. According to a local news site, the man had an affinity for the Tohoku region and had visited frequently over the years. His long-desired move to the area happened to coincide with the outbreak of novel pneumonia cases in Tokyo. A virus was starting to spread around the country and had already claimed the lives of a few notable people, but there had been no reports of infection in Iwate prefecture—at least, not yet. The man from Tokyo had signed a lease for a condominium, but the condo residents held a meeting and decided that he needed first to quarantine in temporary housing—which was this abandoned apartment—until they could be assured he was not a carrier of the virus. And that was where he had died, though the actual cause remained unknown.

He was said to have chosen this town after he became friendly with locals he'd met at the several izakaya he frequented, but those "friends" were apparently unable to come to his aid.

Searching through the night for further details, Shinobu came across a post that said town hall officials had sided with the condo residents, which made the picture clear that Honma had been effectively driven to his death by the townspeople. Was today's customer in on it too? Shinobu wondered what she made of the incident.

"My bathtub drain has gotten... clogged..."

When he first played the woman's recorded message where she politely stated her problem and address, he wondered why she was calling him. She had to know from his postcard address that she lived at least a half-hour drive away. He called her back, and the answering machine picked up, so he informed her of his availability, and in the early hours of the following morning, she confirmed the appointment in a voicemail.

After getting kicked out of his Tokyo apartment the previous summer for falling behind on rent, Shinobu had returned to his childhood home for the first time in thirteen years. His older brother was now the legal owner of the sprawling old family home, and the space he was let to use was the *kura* behind the main house, which was essentially a storage space with no electricity or running water. His childhood room was now the room of his brother's son.

Shinobu parked his brother's car in the garage and disinfected the keys before returning them to the shelf in the dining room of the main house. His sister-in-law was in the kitchen preparing the rice, her head down, lips pursed. She didn't bother with a "welcome home" or a "where'd you go?" And Shinobu didn't offer an "I'm home" either.

He went out for a jog to the river as he did every day, and did not encounter a soul. Ambling down the riverbank, he sat on a faded wood bench at the water's edge and fiddled with his phone. He returned to the house before sundown and quickly showered in the bathroom of the *hanare* annex before anybody else in the family, changing into a gray sweatshirt and sweatpants. He threw his jogging clothes and dirty laundry from the past three days into the washing machine and then, when the cycle was done, into the dryer.

Anytime he used the shower, changing area, toilet, or any other shared space, he cleaned it thoroughly so as not to leave a hair behind.

Since leaving home at nineteen, Shinobu had gone from one manual labor job to the next, working his way down to Sendai, Fukushima, and finally Tokyo. When he was twenty-nine, he met a girl on social media who worked at an art gallery in Tokyo's fashionable Aoyama area. After they'd dated for a while and started to discuss moving in together, a sculpture that was scheduled to be shown at the girl's gallery vanished. It was an iron statue of a dictator, small enough to fit in the palm of one's hand, created by a Polish artist known mainly in art circles.

"Oh my god, it's my fault," the girl told Shinobu. "That thing was so creepy, I would have hurled it at the wall if anyone tried to give it to me as a gift. And now I have to pay for it. Do you think I can borrow, like, two million yen? I promise to work nights to pay you back."

Shinobu lied to his brother in order to get the money, saying that he had scratched up a yakuza's car. But no sooner had he handed the girl the cash than she went missing. She moved out of her apartment, and, when he visited the workplace that she had vaguely described to him earlier, he found that it was a dentist's office.

He'd swindled his brother, and now he had a debt he could never repay. If he wanted to continue staying at his brother's home, he had to obey every house rule, of which there were many. His sister-in-law was the one, it appeared, who determined that his clothes were never to be washed together with theirs.

He used the microwave in the main house to heat up the mackerel bento he'd bought on his way home from work. His sister-in-law continued to ignore him as she mixed miso into the broth over the stove, and his two nephews and niece in the living room were engrossed in their video games and didn't so much as glance his way. Holding the warmed bento with both hands, he slipped into his sandals and scurried back to his shelter.

Opening the rickety door, he switched on his flashlight. He'd pushed the old useless woven bamboo baskets to one side, as well as the wooden chest, broken wall clock, armchair with cracked legs, and pre-flat-screen television set, in order to create a space the size of four tatami mats, just big enough for a futon mattress. He sat cross-legged on the futon and shined the flashlight on his bento dinner, which he ate and washed down with Coke from a plastic bottle. It was a good thing his body rejected alcohol, he thought, because, if it didn't, for sure he'd drink himself into oblivion. He took his wooden chopsticks and empty bento container to the *hanare* annex and rinsed them in the bathroom sink, waiting until everybody went to bed to throw them into the trash.

The payment he received from the woman today would tide him over for a while—a few days when he wouldn't have to ask his brother for food money.

He brushed his teeth under an outdoor faucet in the backyard. Having rinsed his mouth and spat onto the grass, he returned to the *kura*, climbed into his futon, and turned off the flashlight. When he looked up at the ceiling, he saw only darkness, a black so intense he feared it would crush him. A chill ran down his spine. If there were an earthquake of magnitude five or six while he slept, his head would be bloodied by the toppled chest of drawers. The thought unnerved him so much that he got up and turned his body around 180 degrees. But now the lower half of his body would be flattened. He curled himself into the fetal position. It made no difference. No matter how he slept, he'd be crushed, but he lacked the will to do anything more about it. He decided to sleep as he always did.

*

"Isn't that... you know...?"

As the Golden Week holiday in May neared and the cherry blossoms bloomed in full, Tae entered the Yakuodo drugstore past the train station and observed two elderly women whispering to each other. She recognized them from years past. The woman in the burgundy parka lived in Rodenheim, the old apartment building near the shopping arcade. The first floor of Rodenheim housed a café run by a social welfare organization, which Tae used to frequent on her days off for their scone-and-tea set. She'd occasionally see the woman there. This was before Tae moved to Tokyo; she hadn't set foot in the café since moving back.

She was seeing the woman for the first time in over ten years.

The woman in the mustard-colored shawl—Yamada was her name—lived in a house between Blue Sky Dry

Cleaning and the post office. Tae hadn't seen her since returning, either. She was slightly bent over but appeared well.

For people of this town, gossip was a form of entertainment. When Tae was a junior high school teacher here, her mother timidly said one day, "Someone told me they heard Yamada-san and her friends talking about how your classroom is full of undisciplined children. Is that true?" Tae's school wasn't even in this town—it was in the next town over. "Yamada-san heard it from a relative, and..." her mother continued. Tae wished she would stop. What else were people saying behind her back? That she was an incompetent teacher who couldn't manage her kids? That she was no longer young and should be looking for *permanent* employment—someone to marry, in other words?

Tae knew from the banter she'd overheard long ago in the café that the women had met in illustration classes at the community center. She didn't know if they still went there. She deliberated whether or not to acknowledge them, and finally decided to act like she didn't know who they were. Their hushed tones trailed after her.

"That woman. You know, the one who lives by the dry cleaner's?"

She might only have been hearing things, or they could

be whispering about someone else. Still, Tae paused to listen. As she stood frozen to her spot, the women parted before long, waving to each other as they pushed their carts in different directions.

If only she'd been nice to him, he might not have had to die. He ordered those nice senbei all the way from Tokyo, and she left them outside her door for a whole night. Don't you think that's going overboard, even with the virus?

They lived so close to each other, and they were both alone. What a shame they couldn't be friends.

Placing toilet paper and baking soda in her cart, Tae imagined the rumors that whirled around about her. After her father's death, and after she decided against a new cell phone when her old one died, because of the forced child labor in African rare metal mines, days often passed without any human interaction, and she sometimes found herself playing out conversations other people might be having in her head.

Did you know her house is the only one in the neighborhood that doesn't have any senbei wrappers in their trash? She hasn't touched them. You know, her father used to work at the bank. That house. She's the only child. Do you know she had to leave town because she got into some kind of trouble? She moved to Tokyo, but she couldn't find anyone to marry, so she came back last year...

Tae found herself muttering and snapped out of her reverie. She scanned her surroundings, but no one seemed to have heard her.

Best wishes, H. Honma.

Thanks to the handyman's offhand remark about the old man's mysterious death, Tae was now having trouble sleeping at night. Though she wasn't, by nature, the type to befriend her neighbors, shouldn't she have at least opened the door when he dropped by—it was just once, as far as she knew—and welcomed him with a smile? Shouldn't she have said, "You've moved here from so far away. I hear there are stay-at-home orders in Tokyo now, but there's nothing like that here. There are so few people walking around to begin with, what with depopulation and everything. Please let me know if you ever need anything."

She pictured herself greeting him that way. Her, chatting with someone from Tokyo in the present climate.

Oh, you lived in Setagaya? I visited the Setagaya Museum once when they were showing the Boston Museum Exhibition.

That would never happen.

As she reached for the bamboo charcoal soap, she remembered she had an extra one at home. She surveyed the store again. The jingle with the maddening rhythm played on a loop over the loudspeakers, along with the shop manager's voice announcing the day's discounts.

Shoppers kept a safe distance from one another as they browsed the shelves under the pale white lights. It had always been this way, even before Tae moved away. She'd never seen a line form at the registers.

Stopping by the co-op grocery next to the drugstore, she selected some carrots and *nanohana* in the local produce section. She tried to consume locally grown vegetables twice a day, but she no longer ate beef due to its negative impact on the environment. She found pork fat unpalatable and ate only the breast meat of chickens that had been grown on antibiotic-free farms. Her favorite dish was *oyako donburi* made with chicken and eggs from the same farm.

How many doors had Honma knocked on? How many times had he handed out his gift of senbei? She could see the Rodenheim woman in her kitchen, dropping the unwelcome senbei into the trash. Or perhaps the woman would be too ashamed to waste perfectly good food. Tae worried about the crackers themselves, still in their tin containers, which were still gift-wrapped, crying in a heap in the dark: "Please... help..."

As her ears filled with the echoes of senbei being crushed to bits, Tae groaned. Sensing a stranger's stare, she left the store without turning around and walked to her car in the parking lot, now bathed in blue darkness.

Big band jazz played on her radio as she steered toward her neighborhood with hardly a streetlamp to guide her.

The ecru curtains of the Blue Sky Dry Cleaning building were drawn on both the top and bottom floors. The dry cleaning business used to be run by a woman with wavy hair dyed jet-black and her middle-aged son, who was paralyzed on one side of his body. But it had already shut down by the time Tae moved back to town last spring. According to Tae's mother, the dry cleaning franchise that opened inside the co-op offered lower prices, taking away all Blue Sky's customers. The mother and son had posted a closing notice on the door and vanished without a trace.

After Golden Week, Tae decided to walk to the post office instead of taking her car, thinking she could use some exercise. The post office had an ATM, from which she withdrew cash and checked her balance. As long as she remained in good health, she would be able to get by on the savings her parents had left behind.

"Isn't that...?"

She thought she heard whispering and turned to see that a line had formed behind her, with each person maintaining a safe distance in front of them. *I'm just imagining things.* She'd tried to finish her bank transaction swiftly, but perhaps it wasn't fast enough. She grabbed her receipt and headed for the door.

They lived so close to each other. What a shame they couldn't be friends.

Seeing someone approach the entrance, she did an about-face and stepped back into the post office, though she had no business to attend to there. There were ten people seated on matcha-colored sofas, and they turned toward her at once. Some faces she recognized, others she couldn't make out because of their masks. Why were they all staring? *Just a middle-aged lady coming through,* she almost joked out loud, but caught herself and scurried out with her head down.

Cherry blossom petals were fluttering down in the breeze. She walked to a deserted street with a ryokan that had been there forever and whose roof looked ready to cave in at any moment. A notice on the candy-colored glass sliding door read: *3,000 yen a night without meals.* The words had been scrawled sloppily with a brush. The nearby udon restaurant, sake store, and bar were all shuttered.

She continued up the street, which was located at the base of a hill that had a lookout at the top, then turned the corner into a deserted residential neighborhood. She picked up her pace and approached the hill where her own house stood. When she got to Blue Sky Dry Cleaning, she heaved a sigh of relief, and she wiped the dust off the bench with tissue and sat down to rest. *Did Honma ever sit here?* Overwhelmed by the sudden thought, she rose to her feet.

When she returned home, she found the old-fashioned fax machine, which was attached to the house phone, spewing massive amounts of paper onto the floor.

"DO NOT cut down the 250-year-old ginkgo trees for a road expansion plan that is absolutely unnecessary and needs to be terminated NOW!"

"Protect the ginkgo trees! Once you cut them, there's no going back!"

"Send the road expansion money to aid medical professionals immediately!"

"Stop wasting our tax money!"

Message after message in furious scrawls of ballpoint, calligraphy brush, or magic marker from phone numbers she didn't recognize. Before she could finish reading, the machine emitted a high-pitched beep, signaling that another fax was incoming.

"YOU MORONS profiting off our hard-earned tax money deserve to die! Not our beloved ginkgos!"

The machine ran out of paper.

Tae couldn't remember seeing any towering ginkgo trees around the city. But she opened a phone book for the contact information of city departments that might be affiliated with the trees to see if her phone number could have been confused with theirs. The numbers bore no resemblance. Her contact info must have gotten mixed up somehow with the contractors who were cutting down the trees.

A red lamp was flickering on the phone-and-fax machine, signaling that she also had voicemails. "You have nineteen messages."

Not wanting to listen to a single one, she yanked the cord out of the wall. The machine went dark. She looked down at the paper on the floor, wishing people would be more mindful of their language in case their fax was ever sent to the wrong number.

If Honma had indeed died by suicide, could she have been the one who pushed him over the edge, even if she'd done nothing directly? Was this her punishment? *It wasn't my fault*, Tae repeated silently, taking a pair of scissors to the paper.

*

I KNOW YOUR SECRET.
IF YOU DON'T WANT EVERYONE ELSE TO FIND OUT,
GIVE ME HUSH MONEY.
RUNA

One night in early June, Shinobu received a text message from his thirteen-year-old niece with a video link attached. He clicked the link, but it wouldn't open on his phone.

DID YOU WATCH IT?
IT'S TOTALLY YOU, RIGHT?

Shinobu didn't reply, but she texted again the following day, and the day after that. He ignored the texts. Runa never addressed him directly when she ran into him in the house. But she was aware of his presence, and, whenever he was near, she paused her furious typing on her phone and glanced up. As soon as he turned away, she returned to the LCD world in her hands.

As the days grew warmer, she lay on the sofa wearing shorts so brief that her underwear was peeking. Shinobu found himself come dangerously close to sneaking a glance at her thighs, splayed carelessly in front of him, but he passed by her in a daze, willing himself not to look.

Whooooo... chirp-chirp!

Four days after Runa's first blackmail message, Shinobu sat on the bench by the river, listening to the brave song of a Japanese bush warbler, something he wasn't accustomed to hearing in spring. Its cry was urgent and piercing;

perhaps the bird was frantic for a mate. Checking to see that no one was around, he stubbed out his cigarette and turned his head toward the trees where the cherry blossoms had been replaced by fresh green leaves and crooned, "*Whooooo... chirp-chirp!*"

Whooooo... chirp-chirp...

The bird waited a beat before responding in a lower, possibly cautious, tone. Encouraged, Shinobu tried whistling. His ability to imitate the raspy quality of the call—which wavered slightly as it traveled through the air before fading out—surprised him. The bird appeared to have gotten worked up over the arrival of potential competition, fluttering its wings as it repeated *whoo, whoo, whoo*. Feeling proud of his newly discovered skill, Shinobu turned to face the river again.

"Talking to a friend?"

At the sound of a female voice, Shinobu pulled his mask back up and turned. Runa was making her way down the grassy riverbank. She was wearing a striped T-shirt, a denim miniskirt that exposed her pointy kneecaps, and a mask. When she approached, she peered into his face and blinked as though mystified. *Ha ha*, Shinobu wanted to sneer, but simply replied, "Why not? We're not allowed to go anywhere, and I'm between jobs, so I might as well hang out here with the bird. At least it's free."

"You didn't watch the video I sent?" She thrust her phone in his face, with the screen open to her sent message.

"I can't open it on my phone."

"Why don't you buy a new one then? We all got 100,000 yen from the government. Not that it did me any good, since my money went straight into Dad's account."

"I paid some overdue bills, and I only have enough for food to last me until next week."

"Liar. Like I'm gonna believe that. Oh, whatever. When you see this video, you're going to want to pay me not to share it with the world," Runa taunted, facing the river and looking at her phone. Shinobu turned his attention back to the water and saw the mottled patterns of black, gray, and reddish-brown stones, a school of small fish, and a pair of ducks swimming side by side. He wished he could paddle off with them.

"Go ahead, share it. It's got nothing to do with me."

Shinobu felt a tap on his shoulder. Runa had snuck around behind him. She smirked and showed him her phone.

A square-jawed man with sunglasses, a swimming cap, and black briefs is on a beach on a cloudy day. He has a tanned, hairy chest. A skinny guy, in the same get-up, walks up to him confidently, and the two start wrestling in a slow, deliberate manner. Their breathing grows heavy, and soon they are covered in sweat and sand as they strip off each other's briefs and are locked, nude, in a heavy-duty embrace.

"How is this my secret?"

"Gay porn. It came up when I searched your name. Look at the big guy. His lips look like yours. This is how you made a living in Tokyo, right?"

The man, who apparently shared Shinobu's full name, gets tackled by the skinny guy and tries to crawl away, moaning, when the screen goes dark.

"Aw, battery died," Runa muttered as she tried to replay the video. Frustrated, she slipped the phone into her pocket. "I just upgraded this phone! Maybe I got a defective one. Aw, I wanted you to see the credits!"

"Like anyone would use their real name. Never heard of a stage name? And what are your parents gonna say when they find out their little eighth-grade daughter is watching adult content? Who's going to get in trouble then?"

"Fine, whatever. I won't tell the world your secret."

"I told you, it's not my secret..." Shinobu started saying, but Runa turned her back before he could finish. She ran across the grassy field and up the riverbank, taking out her phone and poking at it as she stormed off. Shinobu turned and gazed out at the water's surface, which now shone like syrup under the honey-colored rays. He lit another cigarette.

A white heron fluttered into sight and landed on the other shore. As he watched it balance on one leg and search for food, voices began to echo in his head.

Murderer. Murderer. Murderer.

It was a few years earlier, in late December, when Shinobu was in Okinawa, working for a security company that was guarding the construction of a new U.S. military base in the face of local protests. There was a confrontation, and there were cries of "Get out!" and "Stop the violence!" A woman in pink overalls, heavy makeup, and eyes filled with rage, got in front of Shinobu, chanting and shrieking at him with waxy red lips. She lunged for him and kicked him with her boots before fellow protesters held her back. Appearing to simmer down momentarily, she leaped again, undeterred, her violet-shadowed eyes bulging.

"Step back! Step away! Please stay out of the way of oncoming traffic! Please, you are disrupting traffic!" someone yelled into a megaphone.

Shinobu was a lowly employee who had been sent merely to amplify security presence. The woman extracted what appeared to be a razor blade from her pocket. Shinobu swatted it out of her hand, causing her to lose her balance. When he leaned forward to catch her, she mistook it as him putting his arm around her waist, and in wrangling herself free, she knocked off his sunglasses. Shinobu shut his eyes. Trying to fend her off, he struck her in the stomach. The next thing he knew, she was tipping over to the side with her arms flailing. Her widened eyes locked onto Shinobu as she went down and landed on the asphalt with a dull thud.

"You trying to kill her? Murderer!"

Protesters screamed as they circled the woman who blinked a few times, her brows furrowed. She didn't appear to be hurt. Someone suggested calling an ambulance, but Shinobu heard her say, "No, I'm OK." She bit her lip and glared at him as the women around her unleashed on him.

"Using force on a powerless woman! Bastard! You should be ashamed of yourself!"

"You're from the mainland. Go home! Go home!"

The woman closed her eyes as she was lifted by the arms and legs and carried to the tent across the street. Around the tent were signs in bright red lettering counting the number of DAYS OF FIGHTING THE SYSTEM and, prominently, a drawing of dugongs leaping out of the water. *She put* me *in danger*, Shinobu thought, recalling the blade's glare. *It wasn't my fault.*

Later, a fellow guard who had been through protests like this tried to calm him down, telling him that most arrests were of drunks swinging at guards and throwing empty beer cans. He showed Shinobu a compilation video of arrests, which had tens of thousands of views. Once back in Tokyo, Shinobu started worrying that the woman had maybe hit her head in the wrong spot and now he would end up in legal trouble. But neither his company nor the police contacted him, and he eventually forgot about the incident. Less than six months later, he quit the company.

Murderer. Murderer.

Needing to clear his head, he felt around for his lighter and flicked it on. He brought the flame to his right fist, the one he'd driven into the woman's soft flesh. His skin sizzled for a few seconds until the pain drowned out the voices and he yelped and dunked his hand into the cold river. He began to feel calmer.

The following week, he got another message from Runa.

FOUND ANOTHER VIDEO OF YOU.
YOU'RE ON TOP THIS TIME. SEE ATTACHED.
I NEED 50,000 YEN.
MY FRIEND'S DOG HAS A TUMOR AND NEEDS
SURGERY BUT HER FAMILY'S IZAKAYA IS ABOUT TO
GO UNDER BECAUSE ALL THEIR CUSTOMERS LEFT.
THE DOG WILL DIE IF WE DON'T DO SOMETHING.

Attached was a photo of a black-and-white French bulldog with a forlorn expression and what looked like tears in its eyes. His niece's story was so dumb Shinobu doubled over laughing on the futon. From that day on, she sent message after message with photos of the sad dog, in addition to new material on the porn work Shinobu was supposed to be doing. He replied each time with: HIT THE BOOKS.

If he dared to extract even a little pleasure out of the fact that his teenage niece was paying attention to him, it was quickly snuffed out by the voices. *Murderer.* Only when he lit his hand on fire could he momentarily erase the woman's expression as she toppled over, the disbelief in her eyes, the heavy thud as she hit the ground. It soon became a habit.

"Is there any way... that you can come over right now? I think someone is hanging around my house. I know it's late, but if you can come and get rid of them, I'll pay you extra."

It was the middle of June when the woman who'd hired him to clean her drain called again, her voice strained. It was past eleven at night.

*

Had two months really passed since the day Honma came over to introduce himself? Taking out the trash in the early morning, Tae spotted bright red mock-strawberries growing on the side of the road. She picked a few of them, along with some white and light peach wildflowers that bloomed riotously, and placed them in a vase atop the shoe cabinet.

She was wiping the stairs down one afternoon when the phone rang. She let the machine pick up.

"Is this... the home of... Ms. Tae Kudo?..."

It sounded like Honma's gravelly voice, which she heard through the intercom just that one time. She ignored the call and focused on her housework, scrubbing the first-floor toilet, bathroom sink, and wet room, before pouring herself a glass of cold barley tea. She replayed the message.

"This is... Riku Oikawa's father. You do remember me, don't you?..."

She did. She refilled her glass with tea and sucked on a piece of candy. Craving something salty next, she chewed on some *iriko*.

"There is something I need to speak to you about. In person, if you're home, perhaps sometime next week. I hear... you're back in town. You moved to the city after you quit teaching here and got a new job. You last lived in Saitama, and you moved back here because your apartment was being torn down and you received compensation from the realtor..."

He was right. Though people assumed she had moved to Tokyo, the truth was that, over the course of nine years, she had lived only in the suburbs, in Tokyo's neighboring prefectures of Kanagawa, Chiba, and Saitama.

"This isn't a prank call. I'll see you soon."

The message ended in an exaggerated coughing fit.

Tae decided to cut down her shopping trips from twice to once a week. Making a list of everything she needed beforehand, she moved swiftly through the store aisles. When she came home, she disinfected every item that was brought back into the house, swabbing the surface of each egg with tissue wipes and soaking her vegetables and fruit in disinfectant before storing them in their designated spots.

She kept the storm shutters closed and the house dark. One day she was in bed, having not eaten for a while, and she thought she felt a fever coming on. But when she took her temperature, fearing the worst, the thermometer read a normal 36.4 degrees Celsius. She felt as though she was losing touch with her body and started to think she shouldn't stay in bed all day when she wasn't even sick.

When she went down to the kitchen for a glass of water, the phone rang and another message started to record.

"Hello. This is... Riku Oikawa's father. Ms. Tae Kudo, may I please speak to you in person?" The hoarse voice sounded feebler than before. "I... have... pancreatic cancer... but I'm out of the hospital for a few days. It took ten years, but I finally have proof that it was you who drove my son to his death. Ten years. Ten *years*. The internet is so advanced now compared to when Riku... died... I've been able to gather testimonies from several people..."

Tae walked into the living room and squatted in front of the cabinet as the message kept going. Opening the bottom compartment, she reached past her stash of emergency food to pull out an envelope written with the words *To my favorite teacher* in thin black marker. She checked its contents before returning it to the cabinet.

"Ten years... the statute of limitations has run out... but please, I would like to meet you, just once. I've done research on you. The only family member you keep in contact with is your father's younger sister, am I right? She lives in Mito, Ibaraki. Her husband is deceased, her children have all left home, and she works as a caretaker. She says she hasn't seen you since your father's funeral."

Tae had never told her parents about this. The only ones who knew what happened were herself and the boy. The evidence, which she now kept in the cabinet, went everywhere with her, tucked in a pocket or a bag. For a time, she'd stashed it away in her bedroom closet, and then in her desk drawer, but she found that hiding it in the cabinet brought her the most peace.

Riku's father, or whoever now claimed to be Riku's father, was lying, she told herself. He was trying to swindle her out of money or something. As she prepared her dinner of *okayu* and steamed vegetables, she got another call, this time from her aunt in Mito. She let the answering machine pick up.

"Hello, Tae. Someone called earlier today and said he was the father of one of your former students. He asked me where you live now. Did he call you, too?..."

Tae stopped what she was doing.

"He sounded a bit strange, so I told him you and I weren't in touch anymore. I'm about to start my night shift, so leave me a message when you hear this. We can't visit each other right now, but let's both try to stay well, OK?"

Tae finished her dinner and washed the dishes before calling her aunt back and leaving a message.

"Hi, it's Tae. A strange phone call? No one's called here. And don't worry about me. Starting this month, I only leave the house on Tuesdays to go to the co-op and the drugstore. And I barely saw people to start with. Can't think of anyone with less of a social life. Take care at work. I respect what you do."

Tae flipped on the TV to a documentary following a family of sea otters off the shores of Hokkaido over four seasons. She watched them on their backs treading in harsh waters, expertly cracking scallops, sea urchin, and surf clam shells.

When the program was over, she went upstairs and climbed into bed. The sound of rain intensified as she drifted off, but, amid the downpour, she could hear someone walking up from the direction of Blue Sky Dry Cleaning. The footsteps drew closer, until they stopped in front of her gate. The doorbell rang. Tae held her breath in the dark. The doorbell rang three more times, and, as she nervously rubbed the crown of her head where her hair had become rumpled, the phone rang downstairs.

The answering machine switched on. She couldn't hear the message through the floor. "Message received. Ten twenty-eight p.m.," she mumbled, glancing at the neon yellow digits on her alarm clock before gazing up at the ceiling. She thought she heard somebody weeping in front of the house. Or was it the sound of water trickling into a nearby gutter?

She turned over in her bed. *Knock, knock.* Two short taps on the door traveled through the downstairs hallway and up the dark stairs, all the way to her lying in bed. She turned toward the curtains and heard something like a pebble strike her storm shutters, rattling the window. She considered calling the police, but then remembered calling the police when something like this happened before—the police had sped to her house, found nobody around, and scolded her for calling them for no reason.

She was hearing things again. That was all.

Or maybe it was the ghost of Honma from Tokyo, who died, cursing her for being so ungracious about his gift. He'd gone out of his way to order a premium senbei assortment from the shop in Ginza. Maybe he had a lot of pride. She prayed for him to rest in peace, but then heard another hard sound reverberate off the window.

She got out of bed and put on her glasses. Stepping into the hall, she thought of turning on the light but decided against it, worrying the light would escape through the smoked glass of the front door. She felt her way to the stairs and tiptoed down the stairs. Slipping into the living room, she located a flashlight and searched for the postcard of the handyman who had cleaned her drain in the spring.

She'd held onto it in case she'd ever need his services again. Ignoring the flashing red lamp on the answering machine, she picked up the telephone and dialed.

"Yes?" a sleepy voice answered in a half-yawn.

"There's someone in front of my house. Can you get rid of them? I want you to act like you're my husb—, no, my nephew or something, and then come inside the house."

"Uh... nephew? You want me to pretend to be your nephew?"

"I know it's late, but I'll pay extra. I'm just very, very scared right now. Please hurry."

*

"Also, can you pick up something sweet on the way? Something easy to digest."

"Like what?" Shinobu asked.

"No, forget about it," she said tersely.

His brother's family was asleep. He slipped into the main house, which they never locked, and pictured himself getting mixed up in some kind of dispute at the woman's house and putting someone's life in danger for real this time. A chill ran down his spine. When he lost his temper, he knew there was no stopping him.

But this was a job, which he was in no position to turn down, so he crouched down to open the refrigerator and pulled out a container of milk pudding, which he stuck into his backpack. His brother owned two cars, but the one Shinobu was permitted to use was in the shop for its annual inspection. If he hurried, he might be able to catch the last train. He returned to the *kura* and threw on some rain gear, pulled the hood over his head, then dashed out.

He mounted his bike, which had been pushed to one corner of the garage. Cutting across the street in front of the house, he rode out to the riverbank. He imagined that the river had swollen in the rain, but, engulfed in darkness, he could only hear its roar. He pedaled furiously toward the train station. Turning a corner, he rode past the local Inari shrine and through the rice paddies, then past a produce market with a *robatayaki* restaurant and a Spanish tapas bar. He'd spent the winter working at one of the fruit stands here until they accused him of stealing whenever the cash in the register didn't add up. The job didn't last.

He made it to the station in time to catch the last train. Drenched from head to toe, he parked his bike and boarded. It was the local two-car train. He was the only passenger, but he wore his damp mask anyway. He stood by the door and watched the houses passing by. Dark rice paddies, their edges blending with the sky, seemed to stretch forever, while his own ashen, bloated face hovered above them in the window. He retrieved his eyeglasses from his bag and sat down, caring little about getting the seat wet.

Setting his backpack on his lap, he looked down at the floor. At each stop as the doors opened, the sound of rain seemed to be softening. The stations were unmanned, and no new passengers got on.

He took out the memo he'd stuffed into his pocket with the woman's address, then looked up at the route map above the door. He'd been planning to disembark at the next stop, but he now saw that he needed to transfer to get there.

Handing his ticket to the conductor, he stepped off the train, his shoulders hunched. As he feared, the train he needed to transfer to had ended for the night. He passed through the darkened waiting room and took out his phone. A message had arrived five minutes ago.

"Oh, um, are you driving here? Hope to see you soon."

He was taking too long. Left without a choice, he hailed a cab. When he gave the woman's address, the driver laughed embarrassedly, saying he had no navigation system, so Shinobu asked him to head in the direction of the station nearest to her house.

"Um, toward the hill with the lookout," he said once they were on a street he recognized. They drove past a bank, a post office, and a ryokan lit a dim blue, reminding him of a fish tank. They turned a corner and picked up speed, and soon the dry cleaner's came into view. A bench glowed faintly in the dark.

The houses were dark and still, making Shinobu imagine that the residents were dead. Even the woman's house was dark when they approached. The rain had let up, and he was met with the earthy smell of dirt mixed with lush greenery as he stepped out of the car. The taxi sped back the way it came. From far up the hill, the off-kilter cries of cuckoos rose into the starless sky.

He'd prepared himself for a square-off with a lurker, but he was met with nobody. Using the flashlight on his phone, he took a full lap around the house. He checked the name plate on the front gate—KUDO—then inspected the mailbox and dialed the woman's number. The answering machine picked up, but he figured she'd be listening in.

"It's the handyman. There's no one around, but I'll stay a while and keep an eye out."

He removed his mask and inhaled deeply, then turned away from the house and started up the hill, which grew steeper as he walked. Trees swayed, casting raindrops off their leaves. He saw abandoned structures sealed off with DO NOT ENTER tape, as well as unoccupied houses covered in overgrown plants and bushes. Only one house had its light on. The streetlamps were few and far between, and every other bulb was burnt out.

TWO KILOMETERS TO THE LOOKOUT.
BEWARE OF BLACK BEARS!

By the time he got to the signs, Shinobu was parched. He hadn't brought anything to drink. Deciding he had done his due diligence, he jogged back down the hill.

*

The doorbell rang just as Tae had specified in her voice-mail message.

Press the bell twice quickly, wait ten seconds, then one long press. Let me repeat that.

She'd been holed up in the tatami room where the Buddhist altar stood, sewing a mask out of an old hand-kerchief. She rubbed her feet, which had fallen asleep, and rose to answer the door.

"It's the handyman," came the voice on the intercom.

She opened the front door. The shadow in the dark wore a baseball cap and head-to-toe camouflage rain gear. Small, tired eyes peered out from behind glasses. Tae gestured for him to enter, and he stepped inside and closed the door behind him.

"Did you... take a taxi here?"

"My car's in the shop. So yes, from three stations away."

"That must have cost you. I'm sorry to make you come all this way for nothing."

"No, I'm glad you're safe."

"Thank you. This is for you."

Tae reached for the envelope on the shoe cabinet. She wondered how he would be getting home but didn't ask. As he accepted the payment with his big, awkward hands, she noticed that his left thumb, middle finger, and ring finger were wrapped in frayed, blackened bandages. On the back of his hand was an oval-shaped blister with the gloss of a sakura-colored seashell.

"Did you hurt yourself? Are those burns?"

"Oh, this, right, yeah, I was trying to pour tea yesterday. Ha."

He appeared to be in his early thirties. Didn't young people like him drink tea in plastic bottles? She tried to imagine his bulky frame over a kitchen stove, waiting for the water to boil.

"My hand slipped. But I can still work. Oh, and here's something sweet, like you said."

He pulled out the container of milk pudding that had a red crayon sun on the packaging, meant to look like a child's drawing. His right hand was also taped up, but the damp adhesive on his thumb was barely hanging on. Beneath it, a blister had turned rubbery with pus.

"I thought I said you didn't need to bring anything."

"But I did anyway."

She took the white container, now covered in water droplets, from his miserable-looking hands. She used to buy the same pudding on the way home from work in the city—when she was employed at a government office in Kasumigaseki, at a life insurance company in Shinjuku, and at a trading company in Nihonbashi, where she entered data into a computer, listened to customer complaints, or tended to the needs of the staff members. None of those jobs had lasted long.

"Thanks," she murmured.

"I'll be going then."

"Wait. Let me give you some special bandages that work on burns. I have extra."

She hurried to the living room and opened the first aid kit but there weren't any of the bandages she was looking for. The man was still standing in the doorway when she passed by him and went upstairs, his eyes glued to the floor. She located the newly purchased box of bandages, and, as she descended the stairs, the man looked up and touched the brim of his baseball cap. Their eyes met. She nodded and tossed him the box.

"Hydro... Seal... bandages?"

"Take off the old bandages and rinse the burns with

water, then wipe your hands and put those on. They'll help with the healing."

"Thank you. Uh, may I also use your bathroom? I'm thinking of staying in a manga café tonight, but there might not be any bathrooms on the way."

Were there any manga cafés in the area? Even if there were, this wasn't the city, and Tae doubted that they would be open at this hour. But she answered only what was asked of her.

"Through the sliding door, on the left," she said, pointing.

The man mumbled a thank you and kicked off his muddy sneakers before stepping into the hallway.

I'm about to get assaulted, Tae thought for a split second, her breath catching. Taking the stairs two steps at a time, she ran into her room and shut the door. And locked it for good measure. But she knew that a man of his size could break in easily from the outside if he wanted to.

She waited to hear the sound of flushing. Nothing. Preparing to defend herself, she grabbed a utility knife from her dresser drawer and gripped it tightly, straining her ears for sounds from below. Wanting to make sure the blade hadn't dulled, she laid her left thumb on the edge and applied some pressure. She felt no pain as a line of blood emerged; it looked like strawberry juice. She wrapped her thumb with a tissue. The incision was deeper than she had intended and quickly dyed the tissue bright red. She stared at the wall clock and counted the seconds as she paced the room, going through several more tissues that she balled up and tossed into the trash. Before she knew it, midnight had come and gone.

The blisters on the man's hand had puffed up so badly that they looked as though they could burst and ooze at any moment. The best thing to do was to pop them and put him out of his misery. She heard water flushing, followed by the opening and closing of the bathroom door.

"Thank you. Sorry for the trouble."

His voice sounded muffled as though he were unsure whom to address. Deliberating whether to risk opening her door, she called out, "Please wash your hands with the soap by the sink!" The inside of her mask grew moist with saliva.

"Uh, sure," she heard him mumble. He opened the door to the bathroom sink.

Tae pulled her mask down to her chin and cracked her door open just wide enough to slip a hand through as she called out, "Uh, do you have your own handkerchief or tissue?"

"Huh?"

The water stopped. He must not have heard. Sensing that he was about to step out into the hall, she slammed her door and locked it again. She was playing hide-and-seek in her own house. His voice traveled up through the stairs.

"I'm sorry, did you say something?"

"Do you have a handkerchief?" she yelled back, her saliva spraying the door.

"Yes, I always carry a towel with me. I'll use that," he said in a solemn voice.

Good. Tae was tired of yelling. She stared at the door and calmed her breathing as the man went back into the bathroom. Water splashed once again.

"Thank you. I made sure not to use your towel." He enunciated each word, and Tae felt her tension ease. Not wanting to waste a Hydro Seal plaster on her own thumb, which continued to ooze blood, she unwrapped a cheap bandage and placed it around the wound. Pulling up her mask, she stepped out into the hall and peered over the staircase railing. The man squinted up at her from behind his glasses. Under the glare of the yellow lights, his eyes had a bloated, droopy quality that overlapped with the face of Riku Oikawa in her memory.

If the boy were alive, this might be the kind of man he grew up to look like.

"OK, I'll be going now." The man removed his cap and bowed at the waist, then pulled the cap back down over his eyes before turning toward the door.

"Wait," Tae squeaked. "Those burns... they're starting to blister."

"Blister? Oh...yeah. I was going to pop them at some point."

"They could get infected if you're not careful. Would you like me to do it? I could, if you want." She tried to feign nonchalance, but her voice cracked. She wasn't used to talking to strangers. Her cheeks flushed in horror. "Just need to sterilize the needle in hot water. It'll be over quick and shouldn't hurt."

"Uh, I don't know if it's a good idea for you to touch me... what with the virus and all. Thank you. But if you ever need anything else, please give me a call."

It was obvious from his reaction that he was baffled by this uninvited show of interest from a frumpy woman at least a decade older than him. She felt spurned. He bowed again and closed the door behind him. Tae listened to the sound of his shoes grow distant, then walked down the stairs to lock and chain the door. She opened the bathroom window and sprayed disinfectant in the spaces where the man had been, then wiped down the toilet seat and handle, doorknob, soap dispenser, and sink.

For the first time in several days, she took a shower and washed her hair. She changed into fresh pajamas and went to the living room, where she sat to eat the milk pudding.

She'd stopped buying prepackaged desserts since moving back to town because of the plastic waste it produced. Unlike the soy pudding she occasionally made at home, she could taste the additives as the pudding melted on her tongue. But wasting food was even more unforgivable, she told herself as she polished off the dessert.

She wished he would have brought organic yogurt.

Upstairs in bed, she thought about how to pop his blisters without coming into direct contact with him. She stared up at the dark ceiling and made a circle with her right thumb and forefinger as if holding a needle. She then made a fist with her right hand and imagined trying to puncture the man's puffy blister under his thumb knuckle, not being able to get through on the first try, and gouging it with the needle tip until a creamy substance seeped out.

"See, it smells a little rotten. You left it for too long," she mumbled, then pulled off the towel around her pillow and held it against the imaginary wound. Maybe she'd been the one giving off the stench, having not bathed in days, and the man didn't want to be touched by a woman who had dandruff in her hair. Tae tossed and turned, throwing the light summer blanket on and off her body. When the sparrows started to chirp with the rising sun, she gave up trying to fall sleep and reached for her pills.

*

While the woman went looking for bandages, Shinobu had gotten a sudden stomachache and needed a toilet quick.

Once he was finished, he found he was so exhausted that he couldn't lift himself off the toilet seat. He stared at the wall calendar before him which showed a cluster of penguins—there had to be thousands of them—waddling in densely packed circles to keep warm in a snowstorm. The calendar was from last December. Maybe the woman had forgotten to replace it. The sight of the freezing penguins had a cooling effect on him as he fumbled for the handle and flushed the toilet.

"That's the guy, the one who threw her to the ground..."

He'd overheard the whispers in the convenience store when he used their restroom the day after the incident with the woman in heavy makeup and pink overalls. Whispers aimed at him when all he'd done was follow orders and stand guard so the protest didn't get out of control. He had nothing against people protesting the U.S. military base expansion. He lifted his gaze to find two older women protesters eyeing him suspiciously.

"If anyone needs to use the restroom, please let me know!" the woman in the pink overalls had shouted out to protesters the previous afternoon. There were no public restrooms where the protest was, so whenever a protester needed to use the restroom, the woman in pink overalls would lead them to a driver who would shuttle them to the nearest one. Her eyes were warm, unlike the way they had glowered at Shinobu. He still couldn't erase the image of her petite frame in oversized overalls from his mind. There was no way he could ever be responsible for her death.

She was the one who'd refused an ambulance, and if she died later as a result of the impact, well, that was her own fault. Why was she wearing heeled boots to a protest in the first place?

"Are you talking about me?" Shinobu lowered his sunglasses and approached the two women, who were suddenly engrossed in deciding their choice of onigiri. The convenience store filled with salty sea air each time the automatic doors opened. One woman had her gray hair cut short, while the other wore her brown hair in a bun. Both women proudly wore NO WAR T-shirts, along with dusty pants and sneakers, and a blue scarf around their neck to represent the ocean. They glared at Shinobu.

"All you people do is stand out in the sun all day like statues. How much do you get paid to do that?"

"Are you a contract worker? Part-timer? They skim a percentage off your pay, don't they?"

The enemy seemed strangely curious. Shinobu didn't expect such personal questions. As he headed for the exit, they even expressed what sounded like pity.

"Must be tough, what you're doing. Having to keep everything bottled up inside. It's so sad. You really should think about finding a better job."

Smart-asses. He walked away without a word. These were women who had probably never even been groped on a train. In the company of women like this, the heavily made-up woman stood out like a hibiscus in a trash dump. He wouldn't have looked twice at her on a Tokyo street, but there was something about her on a humid mountain road that titillated him. He was drawn to her, and repelled by her.

Shinobu flicked his lighter and brought the flame up to his neck. He felt his body relax, and he almost nodded off on the toilet seat.

"Those burns... are starting to blister."

The woman had purred when he came out of the bathroom, offering to puncture the blisters with a needle, but he hated needles and scrambled out of the house as quickly as possible. He raced down the wet asphalt that glistened from the streetlamps, his backpack shaking with the newly acquired cash.

As he passed by Blue Sky Dry Cleaning, he glanced at the steel staircase that was becoming wrapped in vines. Had the old man left behind any bedding he'd brought from Tokyo? If so, the room would be a lot more comfortable, even without gas or electricity, than the *kura* that Shinobu now inhabited.

He trod down the street that the cab had zipped through earlier, tapping on his phone. He searched 'pharmacist Honma Setagaya' and stopped to click on the Facebook page that popped up. Setagaya was a big ward, but the age matched. Still, it could be someone else.

The profile had a photo of a man with a full head of black hair, a white flower lei around his neck, and hula dancers on each side. He wore an aloha shirt and silver-rimmed glasses. His long face reminded Shinobu of a horse. The most recent update was from New Year's Day: photos of smoked daikon with cream cheese, *mozuku* seaweed in vinegar, and kimchi hot pot, plus a can of beer. The page didn't allow Shinobu further access. He was closing his phone when it began to vibrate.

I HAVE TO SHOW YOU THE GROSSEST WORST-EVER VIDEO OF YOU.

WHERE ARE YOU? OUT PARTYING?

SCREW THE VIRUS HUH?

A message from Runa. Ridiculous.

Shinobu bought a bottled water from the vending machine and took it into the darkened station building. He would stay here for the night. The waiting room had a roof, a fancy touch for an unmanned station, as well as a bathroom. He could get here in about twenty minutes from Blue Sky Dry Cleaning if he walked fast. Maybe he could use this bathroom, if he decided to stay in the apartment.

Someone was curled up in a sleeping bag on the corner bench, and Shinobu stepped close to see a man so gaunt he could probably wrap his hands around his whole head. The man was fast asleep, breathing in regular intervals.

Shinobu checked the time of the first train in the morning and set his phone alarm, then settled into the farthest possible seat from the man. He removed his mask, cap, and glasses and slipped out of his sneakers and socks, though he kept his rain gear on. He pulled his knees up to his chest and lay on the bench. Turning his face toward the ceiling, he closed his eyes and heard the flapping of bat wings.

The other man stirred slowly. Shinobu cracked his eyes open and watched until the man curled up and fell back asleep. The rain was starting to come down again.

*

The day after she had summoned the man to her house in the middle of the night, Tae woke up past noon, went down to her living room, and pulled the phone line out of the wall. She microwaved a salted onigiri from the freezer and prepared miso soup with *tororo konbu*, then wrote her weekly shopping list. She put on a mask and pulled her hat down to her eyes, then drove to the co-op and drugstore and back without encountering any lurkers. As far as she could tell, she wasn't being followed either.

At Blue Sky Dry Cleaning, a bushkiller vine was beginning to cover the rusty staircase leading up to the apartment. Ants crawled all over the flowers that resembled millet grains, and Tae shuddered, thinking of the conditions inside the room. From the sound of Honma's voice, he had to be at least fifty. Maybe his hair was thinning, and he'd worn it patted down over his head, which created a barcode pattern. If he was past sixty or seventy, his hair may have been completely white, or maybe he was bald.

From that day on, Tae opened her window to air out her room every morning and peered down the hill, picturing Honma as portly or slim, wearing round, black-rimmed, or no glasses at all, with or without a mustache. She plugged her landline back in but didn't hear again from the man who claimed to be Riku Oikawa's father, and the pebbles thrown at her window late at night seemed to have been a one-time occurrence. The man had given up on seeing her, she assured herself, or if his cancer was real, maybe it had spread and landed him back in the hospital.

One day in early July, she decided to walk to the post office to withdraw cash from the ATM. As she locked her door and stepped onto the street, the flood of sunlight stung her eyes.

MURDERER

The front windshield of her car had been spray-painted in black. It wasn't there the day before when she'd gone out for groceries. Her concrete wall was also covered in graffiti.

KEEP OUTSIDERS OUT
GET OUT OF OUR TOWN

The only cleaning agents she had on hand were a bathroom cleaner and laundry detergent for delicates. She wasn't a fan of chemical detergents, but she had to finish the refills her mother had bought in excess. Would either of them work?

She went back inside and drank a glass of water. She then pulled out a dusty picnic blanket from the shed to cover the car. But there was no way to hide the wall. She stared at the two brushes hanging in the wet room: a coarse-haired floor scrubber and a softer one for the bathtub. Bulbuls screamed at each other outside her window as she sank to the floor.

"Ms. Tae Kudo, may I please speak to you in person?"

What if the man with the scraggly voice that sounded a little like Honma had snuck into one of the old houses and launched a plan to drive her mad little by little?

No. She pushed the thought aside and got to her feet, catching herself on the rim of the tub. Glancing down at the drain, she noticed that she'd forgotten to remove the hair after her last bath. A few gray strands. She closed her eyes, stiffening every time she heard a car drive past. There seemed to be more traffic than usual today.

She heard footsteps coming up the hill. Was it him, or just someone who was out for a walk? She heard a dog panting, then a pause. It was most likely relieving itself. She pictured the Shiba Inu-like mutt with the old man who always wore a flap cap. She'd seen them a few times before, always around this hour.

The dog and its owner walked past her car and the wall, then continued up the hill, returning not long after. As they passed Tae's house on the way down, they ran into another dog and owner. Growls and barks ensued in the confrontation. The second pair was probably the housewife in her early sixties with her spitz. Tae prayed they wouldn't pay the graffiti any attention. The spitz was led away once it calmed down.

The sunlight through the window was starting to dim. Tae hid in the wet room until the sky turned amber, listening for sounds while occasionally stretching out her legs. By the time she stepped out into the hallway, it was nearly five o'clock.

She went outside. The graffiti was still there.

She ran down the hill and turned the corner without looking at Blue Sky Dry Cleaning, then headed for the post office with her shoulders hunched. She withdrew some cash and arrived at the train station. Trains headed in either direction had just left the station, so she started to walk along the tracks in the inbound direction, along the sunset-hued daylilies that bloomed furiously. It was dark by the time she reached the next station, and, seeing the light in the vacant waiting room, she decided to take a short break.

She got up and started walking to yet the next station, arriving several minutes ahead of the next inbound train. Seeing people lingering in the waiting room and on the platform, she decided to wander around the neighborhood until the train came. Crossing the tracks, she saw a temple with a weeping cherry tree on her right, and a tailor with a tweed suit displayed in the window on her left. It was unclear whether it was open or closed. A swallow flew over her head and disappeared into the residential neighborhood behind the shop. She could hear hungry chicks chirping nearby.

It had to be bedtime soon for the birds. Wanting just a glimpse, Tae found herself following in the direction of their cries. She peeked over the fence of a house and saw a group of cheery-seeming birds with diamond-shaped beaks huddled together in a nest under an eave. Feeling content, she turned to leave, when the front door opened and someone came out of the house.

"This is private property!"

Under the streetlamp, a man in a tattered polo shirt stepped out of the gate, holding a clear trash bag filled with newspapers that looked to be stained with swallow droppings. He glared at her.

"What? Oh, I'm sorry. I was just watching the swallows."

"You don't belong here. Go away!"

He came straight toward her and swung the trash bag, whacking her on her back with it. She could feel the newspapers bend limply inside the bag. I'm a resident of this city, too, she wanted to say, but she saw his eyes flare as he raised the bag again.

"Get out of here! Go, go!"

He raised his arm with the trash bag and struck the back of her neck with it, harder this time. She ducked and ran, but he chased after her, whacking her again on her lower back. When the sound of the railroad crossing echoed and she scrambled toward the tracks, the man gave up and went home.

Once she was safely on the train platform, Tae touched her neck, which had the smell of bird droppings. Her leather shoulder bag with the worn-out strap was unharmed.

She boarded the train and gazed at the rice paddies that stretched out before her, searching her skirt pocket for the handyman's postcard, which she'd tucked away like a talisman when leaving the house. She would ask him to clean the graffiti. Tonight, if possible, since she couldn't drive her car in its current state.

*

The morning after the customer presented him with a bandage he'd never known about, Shinobu returned to the *kura* to find Runa asleep on his sweat-stained futon. She was wearing a pair of pajamas that had watermelons on a white background, and the light summer blanket was kicked down to her feet. Her phone lay face down on the pillow. The rain had let up, and a sliver of light slipped through the crack of the door onto her cheek, her peach-colored lips were puckered.

Shinobu had a feeling he shouldn't be seen alone with her by anyone in the family. He picked up his flashlight and closed the door—the room was now pitch-black—and turned it on. Runa's face glowed in a circle of light. Her mask was pulled down to her chin.

Should he give her a nudge? He thought, then stopped. He gazed up at the ceiling and took a deep breath.

"Uncle? What time is it?" Runa cracked open one eye. She yawned and sat up. "Why are you in a raincoat? Is that supposed to protect you? You paranoid or something?"

"I spent the night at karaoke with a friend," he said.

"Liar. You have no friends here."

"Hey, how'd you know? It was a solo karaoke all-nighter."

Runa didn't seem amused or interested as she pulled up her mask and crossed her legs on the futon. She toyed with her phone. Get out, he wanted to say.

"Hey," she whispered. "So I was doing some research on Okinawa for my social studies homework. Did you beat up some woman protesting over there? That's so evil."

"The farthest south I've ever been is Kumamoto. Visiting a friend from Tokyo who was born and raised there."

"But what about this video then, huh?"

She held up her phone, which showed several men in blue uniforms facing the protesters. Whoever shot the video appeared to be part of the protest, as they shoved and were shoved in return, which caused the camera to shake violently. It made Shinobu dizzy. The sky was clear and blue, while a cloud of dust covered the ground.

The camera swung left and right, and suddenly it zeroed in on a security guard's white-gloved hand striking the stomach of a protester in pink overalls. The camera alternated between the woman as she fell to the ground, her long hair flying, and Shinobu, who stood stupidly with his mouth half-open. It was him all right.

The video then moved over to the woman as she was being tended to by fellow protesters. Her closed eyelids looked to Shinobu like that of a dead bird. Over the commotion, a voice began to narrate:

"Amateur birdwatcher Ayuko Nakamura, who was in Okinawa to study the behavior of the Okinawan woodpecker, an endangered species, was taken to the hospital one month after this incident for an injury to the brain. She has since died. This is the man who assaulted her and threw her to the ground. He works for..."

"That's not me. The guy is way bigger. And I don't work for that company."

The air was getting thick in the *kura*, and Shinobu's scalp started to itch. He was about to take his cap off, but he didn't want his niece to see his nasty, puffy face. Last night, he'd had a nightmare and fallen off the bench, smacking his face on the ground and ending up with a black eye and swollen cheek.

"Liar. If you don't give me money, I'm gonna write to whoever made this video and tell them you're the guy who did it. People are gonna come after you. What are you going to do then?"

Murderer. Murderer. Murderer.

Runa shoved the video in his face again. The fallen woman's hands were out of the frame, and it sure looked like the video had been edited to pin the blame on him. But it did make him wonder if he just imagined that she ever had a razor in her hand. He couldn't recall hearing anything falling to the ground.

He scanned the comments. The video had over six thousand views in the span of a year and a half, which was more than a few visits, but that was nothing compared to the compilation video of assault scenes his coworker had shown him. What a pointless death, he thought, if she really did die.

"A brain injury one month after the incident? Like that's believable. Let people come after me, I don't care."

"So that's how you're gonna be. I still need 30,000 yen to help save my friend's dog. What do I have to do for you to give me the money? Want to see my boobs?"

"No! Never. But..."

She could pop my blister. He had rebandaged his fingers in the station bathroom that morning but was scared to touch his thumb, which was in the worst shape. He remembered the woman said it could get infected. He spread his right hand, which was covered in Hydro Seal bandages, and put it in front of Runa's face, then flipped it over and showed her the other side. She stopped mid-blackmail and stared.

"What happened to you?"

"Burned my hands. I was eating instant ramen by the river and got attacked by a crow. Spilled hot soup all over myself. See this puffy one? I tried to poke it with a needle but I couldn't get the angle right."

He peeled the sodden bandage from his thumb to reveal a light blue-green blister that had puffed up to the size of a navy bean. Runa looked at his other hand.

"You burned both hands? Ow."

"This one's from a chemical at work. Five thousand yen if you help me get the fluid out."

Runa went straight to her phone to look up how to do it. She nodded, then scampered over to the house in her sandals, leaving the door open. She came back with a sewing kit and a lighter that was used for the candle on the Buddhist altar. She slammed the door shut.

"You're supposed to sterilize the needle with a lighter. Wonder if this'll work."

"I have my lighter right here."

The two sat facing each other on the musty sheets, the flashlight perched between them. Sitting in a dark room surrounded by old chests, dusty baskets, and broken electronics, the scene between them was almost dreamlike. A child playing hide-and-seek could be forgotten in here.

"OK, I'm going to sterilize it now," Runa declared, pinching the needle with her left thumb and ring finger like she was making a fox hand shadow on the wall, then flicking on her lighter. She placed the tip of the silver needle over the roaring blue flame, turning it off just as Shinobu was about to say, that's enough.

"We should let it cool, huh."

Shinobu held the flashlight in one hand and held it under Runa's face. Her eyes were crossed as she waved the needle in the air. Her hair, which smelled like vanilla ice cream, and her forehead, dotted with pimples, turned a shade of dark orange in the light. Dammit, she was cute. It was so rare to be sitting face-to-face with his niece that he was tempted to lean forward and touch her hair and shoulders. But what if she shoved him aside like that protester Ayuko Nakamura did? He didn't know what he would do to her.

"Runa!" his brother's voice rang out. "Runa! It's time for breakfast! Where are you?"

Crap. He pictured his brother kicking him across the room. Runa clucked her tongue and took the needle in her right hand, reaching for Shinobu with her left.

"Show me the blister."

Obediently, he rolled up his sleeve, made a fist with his right hand, and stuck it out before Runa, who was now even closer. Let's see, she murmured as her nail-bitten fingers brushed his skin. He smelled something like sour milk and felt a warmth spread at his fingertips.

"Ugh, ohhh," he moaned like a child as a chill ran through his body. Runa jumped and dropped the needle onto the mattress.

"Runa!" Her brothers were yelling for her.

"Let me do it over," Runa said, ignoring the calls for her. She flicked on her lighter, but it was out of fluid. Shinobu handed her his lighter. Runa flicked it, the flame came on, and she counted to three as she held the needle over the flame.

"OK, right hand again," she said matter-of-factly. With complete focus, she pierced the blister with a single stab.

Shinobu felt no heat, just a sharp pinch. Out of the torn jagged hole spilled a bluish fluid that reminded him of melon soda, followed by a sulfuric stench that caused Runa to grimace and pull back. Shinobu wiped his finger with a tissue.

"Is that good? I gotta go. Gimme the money."

Suddenly the whole scene felt like he'd been forced to fork over five thousand yen for the pleasure of touching his niece's hand. It filled Shinobu with misery.

"Gotta save the bulldog."

Shinobu opened his backpack and started rummaging for the money he'd received the night before. His wallet was there, but the envelope was gone. That was when he remembered the sleeping man in the waiting room. Shinobu had woken to the sound of the man crying, at around three in the morning. He'd listened to the soft sobs get absorbed by the rain. Had this guy stolen his money?

"Sorry, I was sure it was here, but it's gone."

"Huh? You promised."

"I think I got robbed."

Runa stood up holding the sewing kit and lighter, rubbing her foot which had apparently fallen asleep. She glared at Shinobu, who lowered his forehead onto the futon.

"Like, I was pickpocketed, you know? Anyway, I'm sorry."

"Eww... I was so grossed out this whole time, I wanted to get out of here so bad. But I stayed. To help you. Seriously, you suck. No one wants you here, you know."

"You think I don't know that?!" Shinobu yelled at her, volume rising from the pit of his hollow stomach. The sound of his voice shocked him.

"Runa!" The door burst open, and Shinobu's brother stormed in. The light of the day flooded in behind him, and for a moment Shinobu was mesmerized by the silver dust particles that danced up into the air. Runa ran into her father's arms.

"Dad! Uncle promised to give me money to save Marron if I came here, but now he won't give it to me!"

"Who's Marron?"

"My friend's dog. Her family is about to go broke and Marron is going to die if she doesn't get an operation," she whined, running out of the *kura* and hiding behind her father as though she were afraid. As Shinobu stood and straightened his posture, the flashlight rolled to his feet. He looked down to see several yellowed toenails from the holes in his socks. He couldn't come up with an excuse.

He *could* tell the truth and say that Runa had snuck into his room late at night, and that yes, he had offered to give her some money if she helped pop a blister... But he knew his brother wouldn't believe it. He'd already decided that Shinobu was up to something bad.

"I can't believe you," his brother said disgustedly. "She's your niece."

"I wasn't—"

"Last fall it was that preschool girl at the fall festival..."

"She was lost, and I was just trying to help. She was the one who took my hand and told me her older brother had gone off into the woods."

It was all a lousy misunderstanding. A friend of the girl's mother spotted them and called out to the girl, and the girl went running to her in tears. He didn't do anything wrong. But rumors of his *inappropriate behavior* got started, and Shinobu's sister-in-law got wind of it at a café that the woman and her husband ran.

"And you need to stop screaming," Shinobu's brother went on. "I could hear you from inside the house."

"Sorry."

"I don't want to see your face for two weeks. Don't even think about coming in our house, you got that?"

His brother patted Runa's shoulder and steered her toward the door, leaving it open as they headed back to the house. *I didn't do anything. I wasn't even trying!* Shinobu wanted to yell, but he was helpless. More crap. He was always getting himself into trouble like this. Innocent situations that took a turn and just snowballed and got worse and worse as they careened downhill.

And two weeks?! He had to be joking. Maybe he wanted Shinobu to starve to death. Was that what he wanted? Maybe he did.

Ignoring the sounds of breakfast of the family in the main house, he went into the bathroom of the *hanare* annex to rinse off his wound and apply fresh Hydro Seal bandages. He showered and dressed, then put on his cap and a new mask. He opened one of the chests and retrieved a backpack with a sleeping bag he hadn't used in ages. From the bottom of the backpack, he pulled out a 10,000-yen note that he'd saved for emergencies.

He packed enough clothes and underwear to last for three days, filled a thermos with tap water, tossed in his cell phone charger, nail clippers, and razor, a few towels, some bandages, and his wallet. He mounted his bike. As he pedaled, he tried to think where he could buy a bento that would serve as breakfast and lunch.

He rode down the deserted riverbank, past the Inari shrine and ancestral graves that were surrounded by cedar trees, and soon he was biking out in the open through the rice paddies. A gray heron took flight, and, as it flew past him, Shinobu told himself: I never want to go back to that house again.

*

"Uh, this is Tae... Kudo... I'm at a family restaurant... near my house. I have another job for you... Is it possible for you to come by and pick me up around eight o'clock? Someone spray-painted graffiti on the windshield of my car and the wall around my house, and I was hoping you could remove it. The address of the restaurant I'm at is..."

After the incident with the madman with the trash bag, Tae had walked to a chain restaurant and called the handyman. She got his voicemail.

"I understand if the time is inconvenient for you. Thank you."

She chose the mushroom *zosui* for dinner. She sat there, eating and checking and rechecking her phone, when the automatic doors opened letting in a whiff of sweat and dirt. It was eight-twenty. Tae set down her cup of all-you-can-drink green tea, put her mask back on, and glanced in the direction of the smell. The man had on a light long-sleeve shirt over his T-shirt, baggy pants, and sandals. He seemed darker than the last time she saw him, and he seemed to have lost weight. Tae stood and beckoned to him.

The mask he wore was made of white cloth. It was gray and visibly damp. As he approached her table, the stench grew stronger.

"I'm sorry I'm late," he sputtered. "It's not half-past eight yet, is it?" He took out his phone to check the time.

"No, thank you for coming."

"My car's in the shop right now... I nicked it a little. I got your message and biked over."

"You bicycled here? Did you take your bicycle on the train?"

A waiter with slicked-back hair started toward them but turned around when Tae stood up and slipped her bag over a shoulder. As she headed to the register to pay, the handyman stepped outside to wait.

"Yeah, um," he began to say. "I've been to this restaurant before, and I knew it was kind of far from the station. I tried to get here as fast as I could. I'm glad I made it. My phone's almost dead."

"Well, OK, then. Shall we go to my house?"

Tae had been the only diner in the overly air-conditioned restaurant. Golden light spilled from its windows, and behind the building rice paddies continued for miles. Across the road were more rice paddies, with the occasional billboard for antacids, sweets, and consumer credit companies glowing dimly from the reflected light of streetlamps. In the distance, the darkened mountain range seemed to melt into the night sky.

The two headed in the direction of the town lights,

walking neither too close nor too distant from each other. They saw no pedestrians or cars passing, heard only the sound of the wind. The bag in the man's bicycle basket was different from last time. *Must be for his tools*, Tae thought. As they passed an automated rice milling machine and phone booth on the side of the road, the man asked, "You don't have... a cell phone? You always call from a house number. And today... is this where...?"

"Yes. I'm grateful you came."

"I don't... have any equipment... with me tonight. But you don't need anything special to remove graffiti. Whatever you have at home should work. A sponge and any kind of alkaline detergent for the wall. And a scrub brush if you need to get paint out of the grooves. As for the windshield, nail polish remover."

"Nail polish remover? I have some left from my Tokyo days."

"Just pour a few drops onto some tissue. The graffiti should come off easily. Would you... like me to do it?"

More shops came into view. They passed a ramen stand that was painted red and black, a conveyor-belt sushi restaurant, and an udon restaurant. The parking lots were all empty. They turned a corner and came to a darkened shopping arcade, arriving at a bridal shop that had probably once been white. Bright rose pink and lemon-yellow wedding gowns with puffed sleeves were displayed proudly under spotlights.

At the intersection by the train station, they waited for the light to change.

"No, that's OK," she said after a bit. "I've just been feeling scared in my own home lately. Like I'm being... watched... constantly. I'm probably being paranoid. But like you said, someone died at the dry cleaner's in the spring... and no one lives in the other houses on the block, which means my house is the closest to where it happened. A mother and son who owned the dry cleaner's used to live in that apartment. Sometimes I feel like someone's hiding there."

"Do you think they did it? The graffiti? Maybe you should call the police."

Tired from all the walking she'd done, she couldn't tell the man that she was reluctant to call the police because she was afraid she'd imagined all the graffiti. What would the police think of her if there wasn't any graffiti when they came to investigate?

They crossed the street and stepped into the station. The next train was due soon.

"Do you think you could come with me now?" Tae said. "If you can take your bike on the train?"

The man swallowed, his throat emitting a nervous gurgle.

"Uh... yes, OK. Um, but if I miss the last train home, I'm going to have to sleep in a manga café... Would you be able to cover that?"

"I'll pay extra. But let's pretend we don't know each other. It's not good if anyone in this town sees me talking to an outsider. I'll go to the front of the train, and you go to the back."

"Sure. Oh, and you have something on the back of your shirt."

•

The woman who called Shinobu to the family restaurant was wearing a washed-out violet T-shirt that had blotchy white and deep green stains on the back. He thought they looked like bird droppings.

As for him, in the few days since fleeing the *kura*, he'd been sleeping in unmanned train stations, subsisting on old bread and mochi sweets purchased in rest stop stores.

Whenever his phone needed charging, he went to a hot spring facility for a bath and to plug in his phone, but he couldn't afford to go every day, and his body was starting to give off a sour odor. He was glad the woman showed no interest in his circumstances, even though they walked side by side.

"Is it really obvious?"

"No, not really."

"I wonder how it got there."

People were milling about in the waiting room, so they stepped out in front of the station, where a lone taxi sat in the roundabout. Under a streetlamp, Shinobu rubbed the stain off with a disinfectant wipe that the woman carried around with her. The wipe crinkled and turned a matcha color; he balled it up and put it in his pocket.

"I think I got it all."

"Thank you. How are your burns?"

"Better, thank you."

He no longer needed the bandages. The burns had healed and were growing a new, slightly embarrassing layer of fresh pink skin, like a baby's.

Shinobu took his bicycle through the wicket as the woman passed through the turnstiles and went up to wait on the platform. When the train arrived, he boarded it in the back, she in the front.

When they got off at the station closest to her house, she crossed the tracks in the direction of the co-op grocery store. Shinobu pushed his bike through the waiting room, glancing around for the man that he was sure had stolen his money. Once he reached the street with the ryokan, he mounted his bike and started to pedal. Aside from a stray cat, he didn't see another living creature the whole way to Blue Sky Dry Cleaning.

He scanned his surroundings and parked his bike by the white bench in front of the dry cleaner's. No one was around. Beyond the curtain of the sliding glass door, which was locked, he could make out a counter. Using the flashlight on his phone, he walked around the building. In the back he found an abandoned rack where dry-cleaned garments in plastic bags might have once hung, a case of empty detergent bottles, and a twin-tub washing machine. He moved through the items and came to an old brown door that was starting to peel. He turned the knob. Nothing.

He had a thought. If Honma's ghost appeared before him right now, bleeding from the head, he had a feeling the two of them would probably get along. Shinobu was a guy who may have killed an unarmed woman, having imagined she had a razor blade, and Honma was an unarmed man who may have been killed by the townspeople. They were a sad, unfortunate pair who could probably relate.

Walking back to the front of the building, Shinobu gazed up at the upstairs apartment. He placed one foot on the bottom step but pulled it back when he heard a car approach. But then the car turned off somewhere. He decided that once he finished his job tonight, he would come back here and check out the apartment. Shinobu got back on his bike and started pedaling. The woman's house was right up the hill.

*

Tae dropped into the co-op grocery store to buy eggs as well as organic bananas and *ganzuki*, a local confection, which was on sale for half-price. She hurried home to meet the handyman. When she passed by Blue Sky Dry Cleaning, she thought she heard something stir from the second floor. She picked up her pace, taking care that the eggs in her bag didn't crack.

MURDERER
KEEP OUTSIDERS OUT
GET OUT OF OUR TOWN

The red-and-blue checkered picnic blanket she'd thrown over the windshield had been blown off, exposing the words in full. The graffiti on the wall was as bold as ever. The handyman appeared then, pushing his bike down from the hilltop. He pointed his flashlight at the wall.

Although Tae was the one who'd asked him to come, she suddenly couldn't bear the thought of him seeing the spray-painted words. It was like him seeing her deepest, darkest secret. In a moment of desperation, she flung her arms out and screamed, "Don't look!"

The man turned away as instructed. She rushed through the gate and unlocked the front door, gesturing for him to follow. Once the door was open, she ran behind him and shoved him into the dark entryway. He was warm and damp. Tae entered the house and kicked off her shoes, then stepped into the hallway and turned on the light. She washed her hands and gargled in the sink. Carrying the groceries to the kitchen and spraying them with disinfectant, she gave instructions to the foul-smelling man who stood like a lump at her front door.

"I will clean the graffiti. While I go get the items you mentioned earlier, I want you to bring your bike inside and wait here."

She collected the cleaning items in a bucket and pointed the disinfectant spray at the man on her way out.

"Disinfectant. Close your eyes."

He obeyed. She sprayed from the top of his cap down to his toes, then had him turn around so she could spray his back side.

"Please wash your hands thoroughly, and gargle. You can use the towel in the bathroom."

"Thank you."

"After you wash your hands, please come outside. I want you to squat on the inside of the wall until I finish. Keep watch from the shadows."

She turned on the outside light. With only the dim orange light to aid her, she sprayed water on the wall and scrubbed. When her arm started to ache, she took a break and looked down the hill toward Blue Sky Dry Cleaning, which was buried in the night. The sound she'd heard earlier had to be a raccoon or some other small animal that had snuck into the apartment. It couldn't possibly be Riku Oikawa's father.

Over summer break, the boy, Riku, had gone to a beach in Chiba prefecture, where his birth mother was from, and had been swept out to sea with three cousins. He was the only one who never made it back. That same day, at a beach in Wakayama, five middle-school students were swept out to sea and one died, and in Gifu two elementary-school-age brothers playing in a river drowned. The three incidents were reported together on the national news.

Tae had been on a trip to Hokkaido, staying on Rebun Island, when she was notified of the accident. She canceled her plans and rushed home, a trip that took a whole day.

She didn't understand how the boy could find himself in dangerous waters when he wasn't a strong swimmer to start with. It pained her to think that perhaps he couldn't say no to his cousins, who wanted to swim farther out, where the current was strong.

There were over 1,500 drownings around the country that year, seventy of which were children. So many lives lost, and there wasn't even a tsunami. Most of them could have been saved if they had followed two rules: Don't leave the swimming area. Don't swim in bad weather.

"I'm not able to talk... about Riku... right now. Ms. Kudo... he had you only for a semester...but thank you."

When she and the principal went to pay their respects to the boy's father, he had bowed his head, his eyes empty and dry. With his son, he had moved back to his hometown in Iwate prefecture when the boy was in the fourth grade. The father had gotten a job as a salesman at a local funeral home. He married his second wife, a nurse.

Together they had a boy, who was now of preschool age, and a baby girl. Riku was a big boy and was often left to fend for himself, which meant that his school uniform and gym clothes were always a bit stained and dirty. He was frequently made the butt of his classmates' jokes. To Tae, however, the clowning around appeared to be a playful form of communication.

She kept telling herself that if the boy had swum out to sea, perhaps lured by the idea of death, it was because of how his stepmother had treated him.

Since Tae had herself returned to Iwate, she felt a yearning to see the ocean once every season. She wasn't confident enough in her driving to go out to the coast alone, so she always took the train, a two-hour ride. She would then rent a bicycle and pedal toward the shore, where the construction of a massive seawall was underway. She occasionally came upon a deteriorating apartment building with only its frame intact—the first floor washed away—or mud-stained, dilapidated houses that tilted to one side. Riding with the sea air on her face, she repeated, like a mantra, the dates on which tsunamis had devastated the area since the Meiji era: June 15th, 1896. March 3rd, 1933. March 11th, 2011.

When she biked up the hill and gazed out at the sparkling blue sea, she sometimes felt Riku Oikawa's death as indistinguishable from the countless people who had been washed away there. And for a moment, whatever was lodged in her chest dissolved.

Last fall, following her father's funeral, she had gone to the ocean, and, on the way home that night, the train appeared to roll over a large soft object as it passed through the mountains. The air shuddered as the impact spread through the train, shaking the window, the floor, and the table that held Tae's thermos. A siren went off, and the train screeched to a stop. An announcement immediately followed: "We seem to have encountered... a deer. Thank you for your patience while we look into the matter."

Tae took a sip of the slightly sweet, lukewarm mugwort tea she'd been carrying around and peered out the window. All she saw was darkness. Not a house light to be seen in their shrouded surroundings.

The conductor and train operator headed outside with a large silver vinyl sheet to cover the deer, which had likely died before it could let out so much as a cry. The woman in the seat diagonally behind Tae spoke shakily into her phone, "Uh, yes, I might not be getting in until tomorrow." It was starting to get late, and there was no guarantee the passengers would make the connection to the last Tokyo-bound shinkansen of the day.

The ten other passengers in the car appeared resigned but used to these situations. Most seemed to be traveling alone. Their deep breaths permeated the air, which seemed to have taken on a yellow tint. One elderly man stretched out. Someone ate an onigiri wrapped in nori. There was no use fretting; they were far from civilization.

Tae had become a Japanese teacher because she'd always loved books, but, in the years since Riku died, reading had become impossible. Which, to her, might be the greatest punishment of all. She couldn't read newspapers, magazines, or online articles, either. The characters on the page or screen became lighter, darker, sometimes blurring, even dancing, depending on the degree to which she strained her eyes, and she could no longer follow the sentences or make sense of what she was reading. She couldn't read during her train commute in Tokyo, and she no longer took books with her on her trips to the sea.

Unable now to take in new information, she found herself recalling stories and words that she'd read in the past. On the train that night, she drifted in and out of sleep as she remembered a passage from *The Legends of Tono*:

There once was a boy in the village of Aozasa. He was a stepchild, and was sent out to take the horses to pasture. A fire was lit around him, and, as the flames began to engulf him, he pulled out his beloved flute and began to play. The place where he died is known now as Whistling Flute Pass.

In Tae's mind, the boy is wearing a frayed navy *kongasuri* kimono. He is playing the flute as flames surround him on a desolate field. Sparks are flying from the blazing pampas grass onto the hems of his sleeves, and soon his whole body is enveloped in flames, turning him into a shadow puppet. The boy drops his flute and stamps his feet in agony.

Help! Help! Help!

The boy is crying as he burns. But soon his face transforms into a purple-lipped Riku Oikawa, thrashing about as a raging wave sweeps him beyond the buoys. He is screaming to his cousins for help, his legs are caught in seaweed, he swallows mouthfuls of salty water until, crying and laughing, he sinks beneath the water's surface.

Tae woke with a start, gasping for breath. As her eyes focused on the back of the vacant train seat in front of her, she realized she'd fallen asleep. Shaken, she dabbed at the drool dripping from her mouth with a handkerchief.

There was a new announcement: "We apologize for the inconvenience. We will be moving in five minutes."

And relief in the voice of the woman diagonally behind her: "We may be able to make it tonight after all."

According to Tae's watch, an hour had passed since the incident. The two-car train started to inch forward in the dark, and Tae took a sip of her tea—more tepid and unsavory than before—and told herself, *I'm not to blame.* If somebody had forced Riku out into the open sea, it was his stepmother, who less than six months after the accident left Riku's father and took the children back to her hometown in northern Iwate.

I didn't kill anybody.

Having managed to remove the graffiti from the wall, Tae opened the front door to get the materials needed to clean her windshield. She heard a sniffle and turned around. The man was crouched low with both knees on the ground, his eyes on the wall. He turned to her with bleary eyes. "Um... may I... have some water, please?"

Tae nodded and headed to the kitchen to fill a jar with tap water and ice. She scanned the cupboard until her eyes landed on her father's old teacup, which she'd been meaning to throw out. She took it with her and handed it to him.

"I don't have any bottled water. Here you go."

"Thank you. Also... the bathroom?"

"You know where it is. Go right ahead."

He didn't have to ask permission, she thought, surprised, and watched as he stood unsteadily and gave her a small bow. "Sorry, thank you," he said, brushing the dirt off his clothes.

MURDERER. Using a tissue dampened with nail polish remover, she started rubbing the word out. By the time she got the graffiti removed, she felt dizzy from the fumes, and she tottered back to the house. The man had resumed his crouching position by the wall. "I'm done," Tae said as she passed by him. She entered the house and saw that it was past midnight. How long had she been out there, madly scrubbing?

"It's too late for the last train," she called out to the man's back.

"Yes," he replied flatly without turning around.

"That manga café you said you were going to... Is it open twenty-four hours?"

"No...it closed down. I, uh, actually spent the night in the station last month..."

She knew there were no manga cafés in the area.

"I... have an extra futon," she said. "Would you like to sleep here?"

"Is that OK?... That would be great."

"Sorry it took me so long to get the paint off. It must have been painful crouching and not doing anything else."

"I used to work as a security guard. So I'm used to the waiting. I also did some stretches when you weren't looking."

Like the old man on the train. Tae almost laughed. She called him inside and locked the door, then stepped through the sliding door into the bathroom changing area and selected a few ratty towels, which she placed in a basket for him to use. When she returned to the hall-way, the man was still facing the door, swinging his arms to loosen his shoulders. Tae retreated to the living room and called out, "Do you... want to wear my late father's... underwear and pajamas?"

"Thank you."

"I'll go get them. Please feel free to use the shower."

*

The woman had contacted Shinobu for the first time in about two weeks to ask him to clean some graffiti, but, when he got to her house, she ordered him to hide behind a wall. He did exactly as he was told. Anything for the money. He asked for water midway through, which refreshed him somewhat.

If he went back to the *kura* and Runa came around asking for money again, he might put his hands around her throat and strangle her. Either that, or he'd run out to the riverbank to keep from acting on his desires, douse his clothes with gasoline, and set himself on fire. There were worse things than sitting behind a wall for hours, watching out for whatever it was the woman was afraid of.

When she was finished doing her deed, Shinobu entered the house as told and headed to the shower. He wanted to leave before dawn the next morning so he could check the upstairs apartment at Blue Sky Dry Cleaning. He started to disrobe when the woman spoke hesitantly, with only a sliding door between them. "I'm leaving a bag out here in the hallway. Can you put your clothes in the bag when you're done?"

"Oh, right. Dirty clothes. Got it."

"And I've laid out a futon in the altar... room... across the hall from the bathroom."

She said "altar... room" as if she needed to think about it. In the shower, he washed his body and underwear and repeated the phrase. "Altar... room."

When he got out, he dried himself with the towel she'd left in the basket and put on the underwear and soft, blue-striped pajamas that felt like they were made of gauze. He hadn't worn pajamas since he was a child. He felt as though he'd been reborn. In the mirror, without his cap, glasses, and mask, he saw that his cheeks had hollowed and the mosquito bites by his eyes, nose, and mouth looked like red polka dots. But the sight of the infected, oozing gash on his left arm, the result of his bike skidding across the road in the rain, pulled him back to reality. He needed another sterilized needle and more high-quality bandages, or it would get worse. He started to slide the door open.

"Hold on. Not yet," the woman said.

He retreated to the wet room and removed his hair from the drain, then he wrapped it in tissue and stuffed it deep into the trash can. He faced the mirror again and gave his stubble a rub when he heard the sound of the woman's slippers shuffling up the stairs.

"You can come out now," said a muffled voice. He counted to ten before stepping out. The woman was gone. He looked up the stairs, and she was out of sight.

Carrying the bag with his sweaty clothes, he slid open the *fusuma* sliding door across the hall. A thin futon and blanket had been laid out on the light green tatami floor. Behind the pillow, which was covered in a lacy white pillowcase, was a small Buddhist altar with its black doors closed. A few hangers dangled from the curtain rod, and Shinobu didn't know whether they had always been there, or if they'd been put there for his use. He grabbed one and hung the underwear that he had washed in the shower.

On the floor next to the futon were a fan and reading light, along with *ganzuki*, a banana, some brown sugar cubes, a thermos, and a note that read:

A nighttime snack. The thermos has barley tea. Good night.
He dove first into the walnut-filled *ganzuki*.

*

After preparing the futon in the altar room and putting together a late-night snack for the handyman, Tae climbed into bed and caught her breath. It had been a long night. Soon she heard snoring, in fits and starts, from the floor below. The snores swelled and receded, followed by the grinding of teeth.

The repetition reminded Tae of her mother, who had also slept in the altar room. Tae looked at the clock by her bed—it was after two o'clock—and decided to take a shower herself.

It was three in the morning by the time she got back into bed. As she turned over in the dark, she heard footsteps trudging up the hill. She thought for sure it was Riku Oikawa's father, who'd snuck into the dry cleaner's apartment to keep an eye on her. Convinced that she was responsible for his son's death, he was plotting an ending for her that was just as harrowing as drowning. Burning her alive, for instance.

She told herself that, no, it was just someone who was out for a midnight walk, but her mind continued to whirl with images of her body going up in flames. She got out of bed and felt her way down the stairs, not bothering with her slippers. She knocked on the *fusuma* of the altar room. "Yes?" asked a sleepy voice, which in this moment, felt like her only hope.

"Um, I hear someone coming this way," she said, and took a breath. The footsteps grew distant.

"Huh? Right now? I don't hear..."

"Oh, they... just went away..."

Her knees gave out and she sank to the ground, her back sliding down the *fusuma*. As her eyes adjusted to the dark, she could faintly make out the staircase railing. The man didn't appear to be getting out of his futon. Maybe he was being cautious so as not to frighten her. She'd gone out of her way *not* to treat him as a houseguest, purposely giving him the chipped teacup and frayed towels, so he didn't get the wrong idea. Whatever the case, she was grateful, at least in this moment, for his presence. She heard him clear his throat.

"That dry cleaner's... Do you think it's haunted by Honma-san's ghost?"

"Honma-san...?" It took Tae a few seconds to place the name. She remembered the name written in calligraphy on the *noshi* wrapping, elegant in a way that his scraggly, insecure voice over the intercom had not been. She'd heard about the circumstances surrounding his move to the apartment, but she'd tried not to think too much about it. "Oh. Right, you said he died mysteriously. Did you mean...?"

Did he think she was one of the people who'd driven Honma to his death? She couldn't help feeling

-97-

uncomfortable opening the door, and she had no choice but to do what she did with the senbei.

I'm not to blame, Tae repeated silently. She took off her thick glasses, then stretched her legs toward the door of the bathroom where the fan was still going. She was stroking her kneecaps when the man sniffled and started to speak.

"I guess it can't be helped. In a small town like this, you're an embarrassment to your family if you get infected, and the town will be talking about it for years. I mean, who knows, there might be symptomatic people right now who are locked up in, I don't know, a *kura* outbuilding or something. I heard some people went to a clinic to get tested but were told, 'Do you want to risk being the first infection in the prefecture?' and then got sent home."

"I... thought that maybe... a stalker lived upstairs at the dry cleaner's."

"Huh? A stalker, like an ex?"

The man made a squawking sound so strange that Tae almost burst out laughing. She hugged her knees, then turned toward the *fusuma* and asked, her voice higher than usual, "Don't you think, when you've been alive for forty-six years, you're bound to have a secret or two that might make someone hate you if they ever found out? Make them wish you were dead? Not that anyone knows my secret, I don't think."

"Yeah... uh, I turn thirty-four next month, so I'm not really sure."

Even if he did know, she doubted that he would share his secret with her. Still, she asked, "Don't you have something in your past like that?" Her voice came out sounding as if she didn't really care one way or the other. The man gave no reply, though she could hear him breathing. Every time she blinked, the darkness on the other side of the front door glass seemed to grow lighter.

Tae turned to face the stairs, wondering if the man would fall back asleep. Tonight was chillier than last night, and she sneezed. She'd revealed too much, feeling safe in the knowledge that the man, who knew nothing of her past and obeyed her every order, would not come out of the room unless invited.

She also felt as though she wasn't finished talking. As she remained glued to the cold floor, the man spoke up. "That upstairs apartment... Would you like to go explore it together?"

She considered it. Once she knew for sure that nobody was in the apartment, she might be able to ease up a little more.

"Yes, let's go before everyone wakes up."

"Is there anything of your father's that I can borrow? Long-sleeve, if possible. And a mask."

"I'll go look. And you can keep everything."

Tae flicked the light on and went upstairs to her father's closet. She retrieved a T-shirt, a pair of chinos, and a spring jacket. The garments were practically new, and she'd been hesitant about throwing them away, thinking that she could donate them to an evacuation shelter in the event of another natural disaster. At the same time, she didn't want to burden anyone with unnecessary material things. She weaved a rubber band through one of her father's handkerchiefs and turned it into a mask.

They left the house while it was still dark out. She pointed her flashlight up the hill, illuminating a two-level ivy-covered structure that used to be a furniture-making workshop. The building was starting to decay, with a sign out front that read DANGER. The sky had clouded over, shrouding the stars.

Today was trash pick-up day, and Tae made sure to take out her kitchen waste. She and the man walked down the hill lined with dark homes and empty FOR SALE lots now rampant with weeds. Her stomach was starting to twist in anxiety from the possibility of running into an early-morning walker, when the man asked, "You said something yesterday about Tokyo. Did you used to live there?"

"Yes. I wanted to go someplace where no one knew me. But... I couldn't get a decent job. It was like walking a tightrope trying to make rent every month, and it got to be too hard. And then my mother got sick, so I came back."

"I lived there once, too. Moved back for a similar reason."

*

In the middle of the night, after he heard the woman go into the bathroom and turn on the shower, Shinobu switched on the reading light and rose from his futon, needing much more than the late-night snack she had provided. With the flashlight of his fully charged phone, he opened the *fusuma* sliding door that led into the living room, which had light green carpeting, a low family-sized table, and a *zaisu* chair. The kitchen was past the living room. He tiptoed through the room and toward the refrigerator.

He found seven eggs, each labeled with its own expiration date. There was one that had passed its date; the rest wouldn't expire for two more weeks. He reached for the expired egg, hoping she wouldn't miss it. He cracked it on the edge of the sink and dropped its contents into the teacup he'd used earlier, which was drying in the dish rack. He downed it in a single gulp. There were two trash cans: plastics in the uncovered bin, kitchen waste in the lidded one. He hid the shell under some vegetable scraps, rinsed his gooey fingers from the egg white, then rinsed the cup and set it back on the rack. Shining his flashlight, he looked for anything else he could eat.

He opened the bottom compartment of the cabinet and found a stash of instant ramen, crackers, cans of corn soup and tomato soup, envelopes of instant curry, packets of ready-to-eat cooked rice... Well, the woman was certainly prepared for an emergency. Before he could do anything else, he heard the shower turn off. He was leaving the kitchen when he noticed a brown envelope that had fallen onto the floor. He quickly picked it up, hurried back to his room, and slipped under the covers.

The woman stepped out into the hall and let out a contented sigh. She dragged her feet up the stairs and went into her room. Shinobu heard her door close. Lying on his back, he turned on the flashlight of his phone and focused it on the envelope. On it was written:

To my favorite teacher.

He peeled off the clear tape and peeked inside, hoping there'd be some cash. There was nothing but a note on a folded-up sheet of paper with faded blue lines that appeared to have been ripped out of a school notebook.

To Ms. Tae Kudo,
This is my first and last letter. Probably. I don't know for sure. Summer vacation starts tomorrow.

I want to thank my good friends: Abe-kun who gave me the nickname "Bacteria," Sekiguchi-kun who let me grip the dead toad, Mori-kun who locked me in the storage closet. And I want to thank you for saying we were all good boys and should be friends.

Please don't forget about me over summer vacation. Ever. I hope to see you again next semester.

Riku Oikawa
Grade 2, Homeroom 1

The words, which he imagined were written with a tightly gripped pencil, hardened with rage in some places, and collapsed and shrank in others. *Tae Kudo.* Shinobu tapped his phone and searched the name. It would divert his attention from his empty stomach.

A Japanese calligrapher and a cooking specialist with the same name came up. Then there were Facebook and Instagram accounts of a college student who was studying law, and a record of student grades one to twelve who medaled in school sporting events around the country. On the final page of search results, he saw a blog headline that gave him pause. It was posted in September 2010.

I am looking for someone who can testify that my son's teacher ignored the bullying that was occurring in her classroom. My son died in a drowning accident last summer...

The rest of the post had either been deleted or was unviewable due to an issue with the internet provider. There was nothing more. Shinobu searched for *Riku Oikawa*. An IT executive, a hairstylist with dyed blond hair, a captain of a badminton team somewhere, and then:

CHIBA PREFECTURAL NEWS—FOUR JUNIOR HIGH AND HIGH SCHOOL STUDENTS SWEPT OUT TO SEA, ONE DEAD

This news article was dated August 2009, but there wasn't any indication that it was related to the earlier blog post about the bullied boy. The world was full of things one was better off not knowing. Shinobu had no desire to dig any deeper.

But then he found himself typing: *bird researcher ayuko nakamura*. His fingers froze. If he tapped *Search*, he was bound to land on an obituary or a tribute someone had written, but as long as he didn't see those things, he wouldn't know anything. It would be the same as her being alive.

Don't you have something in your past like that?

That's what the woman had asked in a strangely cheerful tone when she'd come downstairs at three in the morning, terrified of a sound that he hadn't heard. Maybe he and the woman were more alike than he thought. But he couldn't show her the envelope and say, "Is this what you mean by 'something in your past'?" He slipped it into his backpack. He would return it to the cabinet later.

"Were you in Tokyo when the tsunami happened?" Shinobu asked as they walked down the hill. He was wearing her father's clothes.

She nodded. "You?"

"Yes. I left here years before, moved to Sendai, then Fukushima, before landing in Tokyo. I got there right before the earthquake. I was just starting to work at a paper recycling company in Edogawa."

"Hmm, I wonder what I was doing then..."

"Wearing this mask reminds me of the whole radiation mess. Even in Tokyo back then..."

The woman blinked and nodded, seeming genuinely uninterested, as they arrived at Blue Sky Dry Cleaning.

"I passed by here on my bike one night and poked around in the back to see if I could find anything. There was just a bunch of junk, and a door that led to the dry cleaner's. I couldn't get it to open."

"Really?"

"Mm. I'll go see if I can get in this way."

Shinobu put on the work gloves the woman had given him. He stepped up the rusty staircase as she shined her flashlight from below. He peeled off the blue tape over the mail slot on the door, then stuck his hand in to see if a key had been left there.

It was. "Security's not great," he said.

He smiled down at the woman with his eyes, unlocked the door, and stepped inside. The light from a streetlamp filtered in through the kitchen curtains, giving him a dim view of the interior. Dust was everywhere, and the smell of a chlorine cleanser filled the apartment. In the middle of a room lined with eight frayed tatami mats was a *kotatsu* with a peony-patterned cover and a dark brown cushion. A door in the back likely opened up to another room, and behind the wooden cabinet were, he assumed, the toilet and bathtub.

There was a gentle knock on the door, and the woman came in. Shinobu stepped into the living room without taking off his sandals. The air-con had been removed from the wall, and there were no heating devices aside from the *kotatsu*.

"I thought the town office was supposed to get rid of his things if he didn't have family," Tae said.

"Large trash removal probably takes forever."

Shinobu borrowed the flashlight and started to inspect the room. A few stink bugs were belly up in the sink. There were no signs of recent human presence—no kitchen waste, empty beverage bottles, or bento containers. No animal droppings either.

There was a rice cooker, a mini-refrigerator, and a microwave oven. Exploring further, he opened the doors to the toilet and wet room, where the tiled floors had turned dark with grime and a rolled-up bathtub cover leaned against the tub. The man who lived here must have been big on sanitation, as the shelves were stocked with containers of hand soap and disinfectant sprays, as well as detergents in chlorinated, neutral, and plant-based options. "Doesn't mixing certain cleaning products cause toxic reactions?" the woman murmured. She had followed him into the bathroom.

Shinobu recalled seeing that very thing on a message board that somebody claimed was the cause of Honma's death.

The final room he entered was the size of six tatami mats, though the floors were wood and not tatami, and inside was a bed, a desk, and a chair. The ceiling light was gone, and the floor appeared slightly dented in the middle. Shinobu walked toward the desk, picturing Honma in a red aloha shirt, his hair now gray, hunched over the chair, writing. He'd left a suicide note, apparently, which was how they had ruled his death a suicide. Inside the desk, he found only a drawer key.

"I don't think anyone's staying here," Tae said. "All the basic utilities are down."

"But nothing's molded over. Which means the realtor must come by to air out the room."

"I wonder if they plan to rent it out again. It has this stigma, though."

"Right," Shinobu replied indifferently. Facing the desk, he put his palms together in prayer position and asked aloha-shirt-clad Honma why he needed to move into the condo when this place seemed perfectly fine. Shinobu returned to the living room and crouched before the cabinet. "I wonder if anything's in here?"

He opened the bottom door, which screeched open. The woman shined the flashlight from behind. In the shadows, he could make out several white paper bags. Shinobu pulled one out. The woman peered in at the contents and caught her breath.

Best wishes, H. Honma

He tore off the traditional *noshi* and yellow-green wrapping to uncover a shiny black tin. It was filled with senbei from a shop in Ginza. The crackers had to be pretty stale by now.

"Um, is this what you gave me on that first day?..." he turned to ask, but the woman pulled her hat over her eyes and retreated, trying to keep from laughing inside her hydrangea-patterned mask.

"I don't... like senbei," she started. "I thought it was better to give them to a hungry-looking young person than let them go to waste."

What a creepy thing to do, was the first thing that came to his mind. But no, she's right: it was better than wasting food.

The woman continued to rattle off excuses. "He'd just moved to the neighborhood... I only found out he died because you told me... I had no idea when I gave the crackers on to you... I mean, who would have thought you'd ever find out?"

*

How awkward it was to have the person you forced the senbei on learn where they came from, and right before your very eyes, too. This had to be her punishment for the lack of respect she'd shown toward the gift. She imagined Honma's ghost in the attic, watching from a peephole, a wry smile on his face. "Serves you right!" she could hear the ghost snickering. She glanced up at the cream-colored ceiling. No holes that she could see, just a spider's web in a corner.

"Did you just hear a mouse?" the man muttered, holding the tin in his arms.

"Put it back the way you found it. We can't have anyone knowing we were here."

"Right."

"I'll go back to the house first," Tae said hastily, not looking at him as she scrambled out of the apartment and down the stairs. Dawn was approaching, and the clouds above the town formed sheets of dark gray.

She raced up the hill, hoping no predawn dog walkers would see her. Out of breath, she ran from her front door straight into the bathroom and lathered her hands with soap. Moments later, the doorbell rang.

"Come in. It's not locked," she called out, and when she heard the doorknob turn, she ducked back into the bathroom to rinse off her hands. She took a deep breath, then said to the man, who she guessed was just standing there in his sandals, "Um, when I'm done, come in and throw the gloves in the trash. Can you then take a shower?"

"A shower?"

"Put your clothes, socks, and mask in the pink bucket by the washing machine. I'll wash them later, separate from my clothes. They got dusty, didn't they? And since that apartment was, uh, occupied by someone from Tokyo, I think we should, um, be mindful of what we might have brought home."

"Understood. I did touch the desk and a few other things. Best to be safe."

"I'll take a bath later, too. I'm going to get a little sleep, and then we'll have breakfast. Oh, and can you lock the front door? Don't forget to chain it."

Tae listened to make sure her instructions had been followed before leaving the bathroom and running up the stairs. She opened the window to air out her room.

Eleven years ago, on the last day of the semester in July, Tae had found the letter from the boy in the faculty shoe rack. The envelope had no sender's name. She opened and read the letter. Naturally, she grew panicky and called the student's house. It went straight to the answering machine every time. "Riku, it's your teacher. Please call my cell phone when you hear this message," she said in her kindest voice so that he would feel safe confiding in her. She never heard back.

Soon her annoyance over the boy's obvious attention-seeking lies eclipsed her concern, and she stopped calling, deciding that she would forgo the visit to his house. The boys he'd named in the letter could be rowdy sometimes, but they didn't strike Tae as particularly bad children.

She hadn't turned a blind eye, Tae told herself. Countless times she thought of burning the letter, but she couldn't bring herself to do it.

"Who'd have thought... he'd find out?" she muttered.

The water stopped running on the floor below, and once she knew the man had retired to his room, she went downstairs. In the morning sun that came in through the small glass pane on the door stood the bicycle she'd asked him to bring indoors so no one would see it.

"This is... Riku Oikawa's father. I have... pancreatic cancer... I'm out of the hospital for a few days."

She hadn't heard anything since that message. Could that mean the man claiming to be Riku's father was in a coma, or, perhaps, dead?

Wanting some barley tea to calm herself down, she remembered she had poured the kettle into the man's thermos last night. She placed the kettle on the stove to make more. As she waited for the tea to steep, she thought to take a look at Riku's letter again. She opened the cabinet and felt around for it. Just two days ago she'd held it in her hands, but it was no longer there. In a panic, she emptied out her stash of emergency food and stacked the instant ramen, precooked rice, and canned soups on the floor. No envelope.

She showered and returned to her room. "I'm sorry. I'm so sorry," she whispered to a drowning Riku who kept appearing in her mind as she lay in bed, her pillow wet with tears. The snores from the floor below, along with the cawing and fluttering of crows on her roof, faded slowly as she drifted off to sleep.

*

A. *Yakuzen curry rice.*
B. *Toast, fried egg, and wakame seaweed soup.*
Please mark your preference and place it in the box in the hallway.
The pen has been sanitized.

When Shinobu opened his eyes, the storm shutters of the altar room had been opened, and he could hear cars passing through both the lace and cloth curtains. A note and ballpoint pen had been left under the reading lamp.

He circled *Yakuzen curry rice* and crawled out of the futon to open the *fusuma*. There was a small box in the hallway that had been folded out of blue paper. He heard the sound of water flushing upstairs; a second bathroom, apparently. The water whooshed down the drainpipe that ran through the wall of the downstairs bathroom. He dropped the note into the box and returned to his room.

The woman came out of the bathroom and down the stairs. Shinobu could feel her presence outside his door. According to his phone, it was past three in the afternoon. He'd slept for a ridiculous amount of time. What was he doing here again? he wondered.

"Your curry's ready, and I put some fresh tea in the thermos. When you're done, you can just put the tray back out here." It was the woman's voice.

He brought the tray into the room, sat cross-legged on the floor, and wolfed down the curry. It was soupy, had no meat in it, but he could tell that the mountain yam, burdock root, and carrots had been simmered for a long time. The dish had to be nutritious, but it smelled like garbage to him. Still, it was better than anything he had eaten while sleeping on benches. Almost as soon as he set his tray out in the hall and closed his door, the woman swept down and took it away. She turned on the kitchen faucet. Shinobu waited for the water to stop before saying through the *fusuma*, "May I use your bathroom?"

"Yes, you can use the downstairs one once I go upstairs. Feel free to use the towel hanging from the wall after you wash your hands."

"Can I also... brush my teeth? I brought my own tooth-brush and toothpaste."

"...I'm nervous about your saliva getting everywhere,

so would you mind using the hand wash sink over the water closet? Sorry."

He'd only meant to stay for breakfast but ended up staying past lunchtime. He wasn't sure why she hadn't already kicked him out of the house, but decided it was better not to bring it up unless she did. As he lounged around the altar room, drowsiness overtook him, and he fell back asleep. When he awoke a second time, it was past seven in the evening. The room was dark; the woman had come in and closed his storm shutters, apparently. There was a message from Runa on his phone.

WHERE ARE YOU. TOKYO? OSAKA?

LIKE I'D GO RIGHT NOW.

I'M FINE, NO THANKS TO YOU.

MARRON THE DOG DIED SOONER
THAN EXPECTED.
YOU DIDN'T HELP HIM AND DON'T
DESERVE TO LIVE.
I SENT YOUR CONTACT INFO TO THE
PERSON WHO UPLOADED THE VIDEO OF
YOU PUNCHING NAKAMURA-SAN. I HOPE
YOU GET POUNDED WITH HATE MAIL.

LEAKING PERSONAL INFO.
NICE. I'LL LOOK FORWARD TO IT.

Dinner was a decent-tasting *oyako donburi*, miso soup with eggplant, and fresh tomato slices. The woman stayed in her room while he ate. When he placed his empty dishes in the hall, she descended and took his tray away.

He tried not to use the bathroom when she was downstairs, making himself as scarce as possible. Thankfully, temperatures remained low throughout the day, which meant he didn't sweat and had no need for another shower. He crawled straight into the futon.

He couldn't remember the last time he got a good night's sleep, having been unable to stretch out his arms and legs in the *kura*.

Here, he felt he could sleep forever.

When he awoke it was noon the next day, and the storm shutters were still closed. The house was silent. He tiptoed timidly into the hallway, which was lit with sunlight. There was another note:

I'm taking the car. Will be home around 3 p.m. Does your family know you're here?

Your payment and house key are on the shoe cabinet. If you leave, lock the door and hide the key under the reddish-brown potted plant outside. If you can manage to spend a few more nights here, I have some tasks for you and wouldn't mind.

Instant ramen and disposable chopsticks are in the kitchen, and there's water in the kettle that you can boil for noodles. For lunch, if you want. Help yourself to the tea in the refrigerator, but please drink out of the Komanoyu Hot Springs teacup I left by the sink. Whatever dishes you use, just leave in the sink. I'll wash them when I get home.

He prepared a bowl of ramen and took it into the living room, where he sat at the table next to a dark TV screen and slurped down the noodles. Ignoring the woman's instructions, he washed his bowl and chopsticks. The sight of the cabinet reminded him he needed to return the envelope. But he didn't feel like digging through his backpack for it right then.

With nothing better to do at two in the afternoon, he took another shower. He noticed the towel he'd used for two nights had been laundered, along with another pair of her father's underwear, and placed in the basket. In front of the washing machine sat the pink bucket, which he guessed was there for his use.

He returned to the altar room and did a few push-ups, not having exercised in days, when he heard a car drive up the hill. The woman was home. He had not touched his bike, cash payment, or the house key. He heard the woman step up into the house with an "oomph," and head straight for the bathroom without greeting him. After she'd washed her hands and gargled in the sink, he heard the splash of the shower on the tile floor.

Once she had showered, she ran the washing machine. The whir of the machine echoed through the house as she moved from the bathroom to the living room, muttering to herself as she cleaned and straightened. Finally, she went upstairs. The toilet flushed.

Dinner was yakisoba with canned mackerel and fresh leeks, along with pickled cabbage. Compared to how he used to live, this was heaven.

At a little past nine it began to rain, and Shinobu found he couldn't sleep. As the sound of rain grew heavy, he imagined the nearby river rising over the banks, pouring into town, transforming the house into a boat. He saw himself and the woman being swept to the farthest corners of the world while continuing to ignore each other.

Drifting in and out of sleep, he squinted at his phone and saw that it was past three. A thin line of light shone from the opening under the *fusuma*, which meant the woman had come out of her room and turned on the light. He heard her come down the stairs. "Where could it *be*?" she muttered as she went into the living room. About seven or eight minutes later, she came back out, and Shinobu sneezed. The woman paused outside his door.

"Are you up?"

"Ha, yes. Slept too much during the day."

"Can we discuss... how we go forward? I find it easier to talk at this hour."

"Sure," Shinobu replied, and the woman turned off the lights. The thin line of light under his door disappeared. She entered the room and sat on the floor, leaning against the *fusuma*.

"Starting tomorrow... I want you to stand outside and watch over the house from nine in the morning until six at night to be sure no one vandalizes the house. I can't pay you a daily fee, but I can cook your meals and do your laundry. I don't eat fried foods, but if you have any requests, I can pick up a bento at the store. And if there's anything else you need or want, like alcohol, you can leave a note, and I'll go out and buy it for you."

She laid out the proposal in a low breath.

"Uh..." Shinobu responded, baffled. "I almost died from alcohol poisoning when I was younger and haven't touched the stuff since."

"OK, so neither of us drinks. I can't even stand the smell of sake-soaked *narazuke*."

"I'm good at keeping watch, but won't people talk about you bringing some outsider into the house?"

"Let people talk. I'm not doing anything I need to be

ashamed of. And if people in this town decide to band together and storm the house, it'll be your job to take them down."

"I'm sure they're not going to... storm the house. But, uh, I *am* a guy. Aren't you scared of letting some strange man stay with you? I might be waiting for the chance to pounce."

He sensed her trying not to laugh. Her back shook and bumped against the *fusuma*.

"I admit that, in the beginning, the thought did cross my mind, and I was afraid to be alone in the house with you. But for some reason, I'm just not scared anymore. Not since yesterday. I can't imagine you laying a finger on me... even if I begged you."

She was mocking him. He was about to crawl toward the *fusuma*, but then remembered her expression when she shrieked, "Don't look!" Her mask had slid off her nose, and her nostrils had flared to the size of sunflower seeds as she stared him down.

The woman had bushy shoulder-length hair that she likely cut herself, downcast eyes that bore a resemblance to dead fish, and a figure that was so bony he could only describe her as unappetizing. He couldn't find a thing about her that appealed to him, but who knew? Maybe that made her the perfect woman for him.

Their meeting *was* fateful, in a way. He had the thought of living off her for as long as he could, until it became intolerable.

"OK, then, if not rape, aren't you scared I might rob you blind?"

"There's nothing in this house worth taking."

She didn't seem to suspect that he'd taken the envelope from the cabinet. Not that he could sell it for anything.

"OK... but you... don't seem to work... what do you do for an income?"

"My parents were penny-pinchers. The money they left me will probably last until I'm of retirement age, as long as I live within my means. Even with you staying here. It's for my benefit, too."

"Huh?"

"Never having to see you but knowing there's someone else in the house is ideal for me. To be able to feel the other person's presence once in a while, like a ghost.... I'll leave a note in the hallway if I think up any house rules that might make this arrangement better for both of us. You're free to do as you please, as long as you follow the rules. Starting tomorrow. Thank you."

From that night until mid-July, the rain and clouds rarely let up. Shinobu spent his days walking up the hill to the abandoned vine-covered building and down to the dry cleaner's. He hadn't been back once to the *kura*.

Whenever he spotted a car headed for the lookout, or a dog walker, or a delivery truck from the co-op, or an express home-delivery service, he turned his back until they passed. But most days, nobody came around at all.

When his workday ended, he entered the front door and called out, "I'm home," to the woman who was somewhere in the house. A toy bell rang back in response. She'd decided that from now on, instead of replying verbally, she would answer him with the bell. Shinobu was given one as well.

He was allowed to smoke, as long as it was outside. And if he had any wishes for food and left a note in the hallway, she would go out and buy whatever he requested. She started to bring home bento boxes containing tonkatsu and fried foods, which he enjoyed, and even the occasional sushi. She provided clean compress patches and bandages that helped to heal his wounds. When he looked in the mirror, he thought he looked younger.

Watching over the house under the sweltering sun wasn't easy, but the woman made sure to stock the refrigerator with sports drinks, which he decanted into his thermos. In early August, he received a message from Runa:

SO SOMEONE FINALLY TESTED POSITIVE IN THE
PREFECTURE.
THEIR FAMILY AND WORKPLACE ARE GETTING
BLASTED. YOU BEING CAREFUL?
WE WATCH THE NEWS AND TALK ABOUT HOW
YOU MIGHT AS WELL DIE IN SOME DITCH AND BE
BURIED IN A MASS GRAVE WITHOUT THEM EVER
IDENTIFYING YOU OR YOUR FAMILY.
DON'T EVER COME BACK, OK?

Shinobu sat cross-legged in the altar room with the window open, screen door closed, and a fan circulating close by, scarfing down a bowl of rice topped with a meatless Okinawan bitter melon stir-fry, which the woman had left in the hallway for dinner. He sent back a reply:

I WON'T.

Another message, from an unknown sender:

YOU ARE A MURDERER, EVEN IF NO LEGAL ACTION
CAN BE TAKEN AGAINST YOU.
SEE THIS PHOTO OF AYUKO'S FUNERAL.

He blocked the messenger, and the next morning, his phone lost reception.

The woman sometimes watched TV during the day, but she flicked it off whenever Shinobu came into the house to use the bathroom. She never watched at night, and she didn't get the newspaper. If there was an earthquake, she would turn on the radio for updates and then knock on the *fusuma* and inform him through the door of the magnitude and epicenter, and that, according to the electric company, the nuclear power plants were running normally. Shinobu rang his bell to indicate he understood.

Not knowing what was happening in the wider world calmed her, apparently. And, to Shinobu, there was something thrilling about not knowing when the ground, which he imagined as a thick layer of ice, could crack and shatter, thrusting them into dark, freezing waters. He crawled over to his paper-thin futon and closed his eyes. Pawing the futon that smelled of laundry detergent and listening to the growl of his already empty stomach, he reassured himself that this was not an icy lake in winter. This was the woman's house, and it was summer.

•

It's for my benefit, too.

Tae heard herself say to the man through the *fusuma*. The words had slipped out because, after the man had spent his first night here, she had entered his room to place the memo by his bedside and saw, once again, how his sleeping face, without his mask and glasses, bore a powerful resemblance to her memory of Riku Oikawa. The man's face was full of mosquito bites, and his eyelids were swollen purple as though he'd been punched in the face. She saw the reddish-black color of dried blood where he had cut his lip.

The dead boy's face, which she had never seen, might have looked like this, or worse. She opened the storm shutters and turned away from the sleeping man, not wanting to see his features accentuated in the light. She left the room quickly. If he needed a place to stay, maybe she could offer him the room for the rest of the summer.

Having someone in the house helped to alleviate her anxiety, at least while she felt threatened by the specter of Riku's father, morning, noon, and night.

Since the handyman began living in the house, two or three times a week she had driven to a supermarket far away enough that there was little risk of running into anyone she knew. She was becoming increasingly comfortable with driving and thought she might even be able to take the car to the ocean someday.

By the time the Obon holiday passed in mid-August, the walls and windows of Blue Sky Dry Cleaning were covered in honeysuckle, bushkiller, and unidentifiable other vines. The man continued to be on guard for the assigned hours each day. She never heard a complaint out of him, not even during the most scorching weeks of the summer. Whenever Tae walked out of the house and headed to her car, he would sense her coming and conceal himself. He made sure to shower and relieve himself when he knew they wouldn't run into each other, and he separated his trash according to the rules. The rest of the time he stayed in his room without making so much as a peep. She hadn't caught a glimpse of him since seeing his sleeping face in July.

Now, whenever she heard footsteps, a sneeze, or someone blowing his nose through the *fusuma* or her bedroom floor, she imagined that Riku Oikawa was not only alive but fully grown, and that she was hiding him in her home. Once in a while, she let herself think Honma's ghost had become lonely in his apartment and had snuck over to her house, seeking company. She felt no fear, had no complaints.

*

Several weeks later a typhoon struck, and Shinobu took his first day off from guarding the house. The morning after the storm, he walked past Blue Sky Dry Cleaning and noticed the broken window upstairs. Starlings now fluttered in and out of the apartment.

As the leaves began to change color and the roadside grass turned shades of red and yellow, the woman came down with an upset stomach. She left a note for Shinobu to go to the store, please, and buy her prepackaged *okayu* porridge. He took his bike that had sat untouched by the front door since he arrived at the house months before. It was starting to rust in several spots. His backpack rustled with the small coin purse the woman had left him, along with an envelope containing payment for his work. He rode under a mackerel sky, the shrieking of his brakes the only sound for miles.

He pedaled past the dry cleaner's, through the empty neighborhood, out to the street with the ryokan and post office. Crows perched on power lines, waiting for cars to pass and crush the walnut shells on the ground. As he passed the train station, it occurred to him that he could keep pedaling and never return to the house again. But when he pictured the woman bundled up in her futon in her pitch-black room, drenched in sweat and writhing in pain, he imagined that it could be him tomorrow, suffering from the same symptoms.

*

I'm not feeling well. Please bike to the co-op by the station before your shift tomorrow and buy your meals. If you can, please pick up some ready-made okayu, pickled plum flavor. I don't have the energy to make it myself. The money and key are on the shoe cabinet. Thank you.

Weak from nonstop vomiting and diarrhea, Tae slipped a memo through the crack of the *fusuma* while the man slept, and the next morning she heard him take his bicycle outside. She crawled back to bed and stared at the ceiling as the creaking of the bicycle grew distant. The thought occurred to her that he might not come back. Soaked in sweat, she closed her eyes.

"I'm home."

Despite her fears, he had returned. She rang her bell in response. His footsteps drew closer as he came up the stairs to set something in front of her door. He had bought ten packets of the ready-made porridge.

She later left another note in the hall.

I took my temperature but have no fever, and I can still taste things. The porridge is all I need for a while. I've laid out different instant meals for you in the kitchen as I don't have any cash right now.

The following week, she knew something was wrong when she heard the man running to the bathroom all night.

She asked through the *fusuma*, "Um... do you... have an upset stomach?"

The bell rang in response.

"Please take the day off. Take your temperature and jot it down for me. I'll bring some medicine and water."

36.5 °C. It was probably the fried oysters. May I have extra toilet paper?

Seeing his note, she called out, "I'm going out, but I'll leave extra toilet paper in front of the bathroom. Porridge is in the kitchen."

The bell rang back twice.

Tae got in her car and headed to the family restaurant where she'd asked the handyman to meet her at the start of summer to clean off the graffiti. The rice paddies on both sides of the road were now a faded golden color, the freshly harvested rice hanging in the sun to dry. The restaurant was still open for business, and she ordered pancakes and a drink from the all-you-can-drink fountain.

If the man's illness was actually serious and he died in that room, she would need to go through the contacts in his phone. She would notify his family first, though he seemed to have cut ties with them, and she had a feeling they wouldn't want to be bothered. She pictured herself dragging his body to Blue Sky Dry Cleaning before dawn, hauling it up the stairs. She imagined getting it into the bathtub, covering it with the lid, leaving it to rot in a room that nobody else even remembered was there. She could almost smell the stench rise in her nose. Suddenly queasy, she went to the bathroom and threw up her syrup-drenched pancakes.

Once he got better, she would ask him to leave. But as she climbed into her car, she fixated on the idea of Riku's father coming over with nobody there to keep him away. Her stomach tightened. She could see the father in the black suit he wore at the boy's funeral, trekking up the hill to Tae's house with a red tank of kerosene in each hand.

She drove to the ocean for the first time, returning after sundown. The town was quiet, as usual. Last month's typhoon had broken a window of the apartment above Blue Sky Dry Cleaning, and from her car she watched the shadows of starlings as if they were being sucked into the room. Her house on the hill was still there. No one had burned it to the ground.

"I'm home," she called from the front door. A weak ring of a bell from the altar room.

She peered into the kitchen trash and saw the porridge wrapper in the plastics recycling bin; the pickled plum seed had been wrapped in tissue and tossed into the kitchen waste bin. In the pink bucket in the bathroom she saw his sweat-stained pajamas, which she threw into the washing machine using plastic gloves. The man seemed to prefer handwashing his underwear and hanging them in his room to dry. Tae had laundered his clothes and towels separately from hers throughout the summer, but now that the weather had cooled and the days were shorter, she did a single load of wash.

The man ended up taking four days off from work. As he started to spend less time in the bathroom and she could sense that his health was improving, she began to think that it might not hurt to keep him around until the snow started to fall.

*

Since the food poisoning incident with the fried oysters, which took him away from work for days, Shinobu had come to fear fried foods. On an evening when he looked up to see flights of swans migrating from Siberia, he stepped onto the bathroom scale and found he'd lost eight kilograms over the summer.

At this rate, he might soon be able to exist solely on rice, barley, beans, berries, and grass from the fields, until his body had emptied itself out. He imagined himself reaching a state of mummification.

His face in the mirror looked more skeletal each day. If the woman saw him now, she might worry that he ailed from a serious disease; it was a good thing they never ran into each other in the house.

The next morning, having lost yet more weight, he was about to go outside and resume work when he noticed Christmas decorations hanging on the door. Dried branches had been secured and looped into a circle, then adorned with shiny holly leaves, pine cones, and clusters of golden-brown berries, all held together with twine. Had the woman made it?

When his shift ended, he walked back to the house as snowflakes began to dance in the dimming sky. It was the first snow of the year. He couldn't recall the last time he saw a car, delivery truck, even a dog walker on the hill. The house near the lookout where he'd once seen a light on now seemed to be unoccupied.

"I'm back," he called as he entered the house.

The woman was in her room, probably making mask after mask out of cloth. He washed his hands and gargled, then noticed a piece of paper taped to the *fusuma* written in a thick red marker:

WARNING

I found a meat bun wrapper from Yokohama Chinatown in the trash. The microwave, which I never use, was plugged in. Did you sneak out during your shift to buy the bun? Please don't ever do that again.

Yesterday, while the lady was out somewhere, Shinobu had had a sudden craving for a pork-filled bun for the first time in a year and trod down the hill in search of one. Unable to find a convenience store, he bought a frozen bun at the co-op and brought it home. His stomach could no longer tolerate the minced meat fat, however, and he ended up in agony with indigestion.

"Sorry! Won't do it again!" he yelled up the stairs. Without waiting for her bell, he stormed into his room, yanking the note off the *fusuma*, intentionally damaging its surface. He didn't even have the freedom to buy a meat bun? Was this a cage he lived in? He slammed the storm shutters shut and kicked them loud enough so it could be heard upstairs. He changed into a pair of pajamas and threw on a sweater over it. Rubbing his foot, he turned on the portable kerosene heater and lay on his futon to look again at the note he'd ripped off the door. It was written on the back of a calendar with a photograph of cherry blossoms in full bloom at the Imperial Palace.

Gradually his irritation calmed, and he shuddered at the rage with which he'd torn off the note. The woman would no doubt be the next thing he rammed head-first into the storm shutters. *Murderer*. The word echoed from deep in his mind. He reached for his lighter. He had to get out of the house before his hands were once again covered in lighter burns.

It had become often, around three o'clock in the morning, that the woman, sleepless, rattled her desk drawer trying to get it to open, or slid her closet door back and forth in search of something. "Where is it? Where is it?" she would mutter as she came down the stairs, going into the living room, inspecting the shelf under the TV, looking through the cabinet. He could hear all this happening. "I can't find it," she would repeat, sighing, before flopping sadly back up the stairs. And then he would hear laughter and sobbing in waves, until everything fell deathly silent before dawn.

She had to be looking for the envelope, which was still in Shinobu's backpack. He'd taken it without thinking, and he now realized what he had done was irreversible. Yet every time he thought of returning it, he wondered if searching for the lost envelope had become an activity that added life to her days, and whether she'd be better off if it never turned up at all.

Would the world look different when he woke up tomorrow? Shinobu closed his eyes, picturing the neighborhood covered by a fresh white layer of snow. Winter had just begun, and he told himself it was time to move to a new town while he could, before the snow got deep. He might take the envelope with him, or maybe he would light it on fire and watch it burn. Spread the ashes in the sea.

*

In early November, Tae was driving home from the grocery store when she spotted what looked to be an offering on the bench in front of the dry cleaner's. She continued home. As she organized the groceries in the kitchen, six o'clock came, and she heard the man come in through the front door. He rang his bell instead of calling out to her. After locking and chaining the front door, he slipped soundlessly into the altar room.

After last month's food poisoning, the man's food choices had changed. He now preferred steamed potatoes, miso soup with tofu, and boiled green vegetables, as if he were a Buddhist monk in training. She still hadn't seen his face, but his footsteps seemed lighter, and he no longer snored.

"I'm going for a walk," she called out to him, then, hearing his bell, left to check on the offering on the bench.

In the evening light, the bench had a bluish shimmer, and on it she found a bouquet of white and yellow chrysanthemums and blue-purple gentian, and a can of beer. She gazed up at the apartment, which looked dark and dreary. Animals must have gotten into the first floor, too, from the sight of the shredded drapes.

She looked at the offering on the bench once more. Six months had passed since Honma died. Did someone from town decide now to offer their condolences?

The funeral flowers were withering. Tae tossed them onto the grass and emptied the beer in the gutter, then took home the cellophane, tissue paper, and rubber band from the bouquet, as well as the empty beer can.

When December arrived, a light snow began to fall, followed by the season's first heavy snowfall midway through the month. One morning, before the man had a chance to come out of his room, Tae threw her *hanten* over her pajamas and went downstairs, calling to him through the *fusuma*.

"You can take the day off today. There's a blizzard outside."

The man rang his bell feebly, sounding as though he were dying. He'd stopped notifying her when he ran out of kerosene, so she'd figured he was simply fine without it. At least she could save on oil costs.

As she walked away, she stepped on a piece of paper. The handwriting she'd grown accustomed to, which always curved lower on the right, had become dramatically faint. The note read:

I don't need to eat until tomorrow, or the day after. I'm not sick. Please don't worry.

Tae had felt sluggish the whole day, perhaps due to the sudden change in atmospheric pressure, and after cleaning every inch of the house—aside from the altar room—and working up the energy to shovel the snow outside, she slept in her room until nightfall. In the summer she'd given the man a Swiffer Sweeper and left him to clean his own room. She hadn't set foot in the room in five months and hadn't paid her respects to her parents at the family altar in that time, either.

The snow let up the following day, and the sun peeked through the clouds. She decided to go out for groceries. On the way home, she drove through a shop-lined street in an unfamiliar part of town and passed a flower shop whose owner was a woman around her age. She stopped, went in, and selected three white roses. According to the florist, everything was marked down because weddings and parties were being canceled around the country. "Don't they smell elegant?" the florist asked. It was rare for Tae to buy flowers; the wildflowers that she picked were enough.

But these flowers were to be for Honma, Riku, and Riku's father, who had yet to show up at her door.

When she arrived home after six that evening, the man must have completed his shift and turned in early as the house was dark, cold, and silent. "I'm home," she called, but there was no response.

She turned on the light to see his bicycle by the front door. The rubber sandals he'd worn through the summer were so old they were unwearable, so she threw them out. Her father's rainboots and snow boots, which she'd also let him wear, now sat side by side. She was surprised to see the snow boots had dried already, after a day in the snow.

Feeling an uneasy flutter in her chest, she opened the shoe cabinet to check its contents. The trekking shoes her father often wore after retirement were gone. But she could have tossed them out and forgotten about it. She was afraid to enter the altar room. He might just be sleeping. If he wasn't, and she was forced to contend with a missing backpack right now, she might want to flee the house herself, and she couldn't very well show up uninvited at her aunt's place in Mito.

Was he bitter about the pork bun incident? She only wished he'd eaten it in secret, and she'd never found out about it. She couldn't tell him that he had to follow her rules, or the house might get torched.

She didn't want to admit it to herself, but she understood it was only a pretense that she looked after him, when she was the one being supported and looked after. She wasn't someone who deserved anybody's help or support.

After changing into comfortable clothes, she went into the living room and turned on the TV. It had been a while since she watched anything at night. A special featuring Naomi Chiaki, her mother's favorite singer and actress, was on, and Tae raised the volume hoping to stir the man from his sleep. She hummed along quietly as the woman in the long black evening gown crooned to her lost love:

> *Can you see me*
> *From where you are?*

The man showed no signs of waking.

She flipped to a documentary about the hunting of killer whales, then turned off the TV. She went into the kitchen, disinfected the groceries, and put them away in the refrigerator.

For dinner she made a simple *oyako donburi*, boiled greens, and miso soup with daikon. When she finished washing the dishes, she called out again to the man she assumed was still there.

"Um, I had an idea... I thought I might go and place flowers as an offering to Honma-san. Even though it's too late."

"Yeah," replied a haggard voice that sounded as though it could belong to either Honma or Riku's father. "I... saw... the... flowers... and wondered... about them... too." His voice had changed, probably because he was eating so little.

"I'm going now. Would you like to follow me? We can both pay our respects. I'll leave the door unlocked, since I'm coming right back."

She wore a turtleneck, cardigan, corduroys, and a thick down coat, and put on a mask before leaving the house. Fine silver granules made the snow glisten a pale blue, which in turn made Tae, the lampposts, and the surrounding houses take on an ultramarine hue.

She descended the hill under a dark sky, her boots stepping through snow that sometimes came up to her knees. The chill in the air stung her cheeks, and the breath that escaped from her mask steamed up her glasses. She heard a door open and close behind her. The man was probably wearing her father's black down jacket, which she had given to him last month to get him through the winter. *Crunch, crush, slush.* They seemed to be walking in perfect unison, the sounds from their boots overlapping before being absorbed into the thick snow.

She came to a stop in front of the bench, and he too paused. A sense of comfort started to come over her, and she righted her posture before the feeling settled in. She set a rose down in the center of the bench and wiped her glasses with her fingers, which were wrapped in damp gloves. She kneeled down, closed her eyes, and put her hands together in prayer.

When she opened her eyes, she looked up to see the reflection of a lamppost on the broken window upstairs. Dried vines were everywhere. The stainless steel sink with the dead stink bugs had to be under a blanket of snow by now.

In her mind's eye, a man, unidentifiable, sat hunched over convenience-store food that had been reheated in the plastic container it came in, which he picked at with a pair of black chopsticks he'd found standing in the teacup inside the cupboard. In between bites, he shoveled white rice into his mouth from a white bowl adorned with a pattern of blue pine needles. She couldn't discern whether the man was Honma or whether he was Riku's father.

How many meals did Honma end up having in the apartment? And even if he had moved into his new home once his quarantine was over, wouldn't he have continued to be ostracized because he had come from Tokyo in the spring of the pandemic? In April when he moved here, this town was still frozen over. In this apartment with no heat besides the *kotatsu*, he'd be sitting up in the room alone, listening to the sound of his own chewing, growing more tormented each day.

Roused by what sounded like a child's sneeze, Tae got to her feet. She wanted to turn and look at the man whose face she hadn't seen since summer, to see how thin he had become, to see if he was now a shaman. She could no longer recall his original features. It seemed he now had worn the face of the middle-schooler Riku, or that of the father of Riku, or that of Honma, whom she could barely bring herself to look in the face. She hadn't seen his cap, glasses, and mask-covered face since the night the two of them had snuck into this apartment, and she felt slightly nostalgic. Wanting to avoid feeling anything more for the man, she looked down at the ground. The inside of her mask dampened and clung to her lips, growing colder and wetter with every breath.

"Go ahead. Your turn," Tae said to the person behind her, whoever it was, as she pulled her knit hat down and buried her chin in her scarf. She removed her glasses, which had fogged over again. She wiped the lenses but couldn't feel her fingers, and she took a step in the snow as she started to make her way back up the hill toward the soft orange glow that floated in the dark.

I don't need any meals until tomorrow, or the day after.

He'd left the note in the hallway yesterday, written in ink that looked as though it were running out. Once they were both home, she would wait until he was sleeping so soundly that he neither dreamed nor made a sound, to slip a new ballpoint pen through a crack in the *fusuma*.

Will he eat something tomorrow? He'll die if he doesn't eat. She would prepare food for him anyway, tomorrow, and the next day, for as long as his bell rang. Even if the bell stopped ringing, she would continue to offer him a meal.

The long winter in this northern town had only just begun.

JAPANESE FICTION
AVAILABLE AND COMING SOON
FROM PUSHKIN PRESS

MS ICE SANDWICH
Mieko Kawakami

MURDER IN THE AGE OF ENLIGHTENMENT
Ryūnosuke Akutagawa

THE HONJIN MURDERS
Seishi Yokomizo

RECORD OF A NIGHT TOO BRIEF
Hiromi Kawakami

SPRING GARDEN
Tomoka Shibasaki

COIN LOCKER BABIES
Ryu Murakami

THE DECAGON HOUSE MURDERS
Yukito Ayatsuji

SLOW BOAT
Hideo Furukawa

THE HUNTING GUN
Yasushi Inoue

SALAD ANNIVERSARY
Machi Tawara

THE CAKE TREE IN THE RUINS
Akiyuki Nosaka